D0407110

O DAYS OF DIFFERENT

O DAYS OF DIFFERENT

ERIC WALTERS

ORCA BOOK PUBLISHERS

Library and Archives Canada Cataloguing in Publication

Walters, Eric, 1957–, author
90 days of different / Eric Walters.

Issued in print and electronic formats.
ISBN 978-1-4598-1673-2 (hardcover).—ISBN 978-1-4598-1674-9 (pdf).—
ISBN 978-1-4598-1675-6 (epub)

I. Title. II. Title: Ninety days of different.
PS8595.A598A619 2017 jC813'.54 C2017-900827-7
C2017-900828-5

First published in the United States, 2017
Library of Congress Control Number: 2017933026

Summary: In this novel for teens, Sophie graduates from high school, her boyfriend breaks up with her because she's boring, and her best friend challenges her to try ninety different things.

Orca Book Publishers is dedicated to preserving the environment and has printed this book on Forest Stewardship Council® certified paper.

Orca Book Publishers gratefully acknowledges the support for its publishing programs provided by the following agencies: the Government of Canada through the Canada Book Fund and the Canada Council for the Arts, and the Province of British Columbia through the BC Arts Council and the Book Publishing Tax Credit.

Cover images by iStock.com and Shutterstock.com
Design by Rachel Page
Author photo by Sofia Kinachtchouk

ORCA BOOK PUBLISHERS
www.orcabook.com

Printed and bound in Canada.

20 19 18 17 • 4 3 2 1

I'd like to thank and acknowledge my daughter, Christina Arseneau for her assistance with all matters involving social media, going through the first draft, keeping me 'up to date' and arranging for all of Sophie's social media platforms.

DAY 1

My senior year. It was over. Finished.

"Sophie, we're done!" Ella yelled as she wrapped her arms around me in a big hug.

"It feels good," I said.

"Then smile!"

I smiled and hugged her back. I was glad to be finished, and I was looking forward to the summer, but transitions—even good ones—made me uneasy.

Around us, the hall was filled with an excited sea of students. High fives, hugs and tears and screams, papers tossed into the air showering down, and not a teacher in sight to mark the last bell on the last day of school.

"It's official, we're high school graduates!" Ella exclaimed.

"You make it sound like this was a surprise."

"Not a surprise but still spectacular! High school is done, and summer awaits us!"

Ella had been my best friend from seventh grade on. She always spoke in rapid bursts, usually ending in an exclamation mark. It was one of her best features. And one of her most annoying ones. Not that I'd ever let her know I felt that way.

"Hey, Soph, hey, Ella," Luke said as he joined us.

I threw an arm around him. He'd been my boyfriend for part of my junior year and through the entire senior year. Ella didn't like him and wasn't afraid to say that to me—or to him. She didn't care what he thought of her. She was fearless about things like that. Again, both refreshing and at times annoying.

"Can we talk?" Luke asked me.

"Sure."

"Privately."

I looked at Ella. "Hey, no worries," she said. "I'm always willing to go someplace where Luke is not."

"Charming, as always," Luke said.

"Not trying, as always." Ella walked away and joined in the celebration around us.

Luke took me by the hand and led me into an empty classroom, closing the door behind us. I could still hear the celebration outside.

"I'm not sure how to say this," Luke said.

"What are you trying to do, break up with me?" I joked.

And then I saw the look on his face, and I stopped smiling.

"You're breaking up with me?"

He nodded. "I've wanted to tell you for a while, but there just wasn't—"

"You've wanted to break up with me for a while?"

"I've been thinking about it for a few weeks, but I was waiting for the right time," he said.

"And you thought *this* was it?"

"Maybe there isn't a good time, but I ran out of time."

"But I don't understand. Why do you want to break up with me?"

"I don't know."

"Of course you know. Is there somebody else?" I demanded.

"No, of course not!"

"You're not going to give me that old *it's not you, it's me* line, are you?"

"Oh no," he said, shaking his head. "It's definitely you."

"What?"

"It's you. It's definitely you."

I felt like I'd been kicked in the stomach.

"Look, Sophie, you're smart and nice and really good-looking and—"

"Sounds like three *great* reasons to break up with me."

"You're not making this easy."

"I'm not trying to make it easy. Just tell me why."

He went to take my hand, and I shook it away.

"Just tell me."

"It's just that I feel like I've spent the last year—"

"Last fourteen months."

"Last fourteen months," he said and shook his head. "Thanks so much for correcting me on that too."

"Are you breaking up with me because I correct you sometimes?" I asked.

"First off, you correct me *all* the time, and second, that isn't the reason."

"Then what is?"

"It's just that it's like you're much older than eighteen."

"So I'm mature."

"It's less like you're mature and more like you're *old*," he said.

"You're three weeks older than me," I pointed out.

"But it's like you're a lot older. Thirty years older."

"Now you're just being ridiculous."

"Am I? I can always predict exactly what you're going to do."

"So you want unpredictable, do you?" I reached over and with both hands mussed up his precious hair.

"Stop that!" he said as he jumped backward and tried to straighten his hair.

He seemed more upset about his hair than about breaking up with me. Ella had always said that Luke would never care for anybody as much as he cared for his hair, and it looked like she was right about that. And maybe lots of other things about him.

"I bet you didn't see that coming," I said angrily.

He laughed. "Maybe not, but I bet you didn't see *this* coming."

I hadn't. I always needed to know what was coming up, what was happening next. I hated being surprised, and this was more than that—it was a shock.

"Look, Sophie, it's just that I want to have some fun."

"And I'm not fun?"

"Sophie, you never want to try anything new, or different, or exciting, or dangerous. You're just, well, so predictable that you're boring."

"If I'm so boring, why didn't you break up with me months ago?"

"At first I didn't want to interfere with the prom."

"I think we both could have found somebody else to go with," I said.

"Then there were final exams."

"So you were too busy studying to break up with me?" I asked.

"*You* were too busy studying. You were *always* studying."

"And you thought I cared more about school than you?" Was that it? He felt like he was in second place?

"No, of course not. I knew you had to keep up your marks to maintain your scholarship offers."

"So you didn't break up with me then because you were being considerate of my marks staying up?" I asked. "Am I supposed to believe you were doing me a favor by staying with me?"

He shrugged. "You *did* ace them. You *are* going on a full scholarship."

I had already accepted an academic scholarship, but I'd have received less money if my marks had gone down. Even without that consideration, though, I'd wanted—*needed*—to have top marks.

"Wait. Exams were over three weeks ago, so what stopped you from telling me then?"

He looked embarrassed. "I guess I didn't want to face you every day after that."

"Am I that scary?"

Luke nodded. "Yeah, you are."

I hadn't expected that as an answer.

"Then how are you going to face me next year? We're going to the same college, unless you're so afraid of me that you applied to go someplace else."

"Here we shared two classes, and our lockers were only three spots apart. At college there are twenty-five thousand students, and the campus is huge. We might never even see each other."

"Something to look forward to."

"Look, Soph, let's not make this any harder. There's no point in talking anymore. I'm going out with my friends to celebrate."

"I'm glad you can celebrate breaking up with me."

"I'm going to celebrate the end of school. I'm free—I guess in more ways than one. Have yourself a good summer."

Luke turned and walked out, closing the door behind him. I could still hear the celebration going on in the hallway. It wasn't just his friends out there but also mine. What would I say to them? What would they think? How could I face them?

The door started to open. Was he coming back to tell me he'd changed his mind? No, it was Ella. One look told me she already knew. She came over and gave me a big hug.

"You're better off without him."

I worked hard not to cry. I didn't want to lose control—I didn't want to let it or *him* get to me.

"What do you say we get out of here and get some ice cream?" she asked.

I couldn't help but laugh. "You really do think ice cream is the answer to everything, don't you?"

"I don't *think*. I *know*."

❖ ❖ ❖

We slipped through the crowd without having to say much to anybody. Everybody seemed to know already what had happened. I was trending. Luke was probably posting photos of his freedom celebration on Instagram. I was only on Facebook, and I never looked at it. Ella would report back soon enough about how this was playing out on all the social media.

It was a relief driving away from the school. It was like I was leaving behind a bad memory. Is that what Luke had done? Had he managed to wreck my memories of high school?

"You know I never liked him," Ella said.

"You always made that clear."

"Remember, any guy who has that many hair-care products is not somebody a girl should want to be with. Guys like him should come with a warning label. *Beware—danger of over-involvement with my hair, unable to become involved in a meaningful relationship with another person.*"

"I'm not sure if I'm supposed to be encouraged or upset that he likes his hair better than he liked me," I said.

"Don't take it personally. I'm positive he likes his hair more than he likes his friends or family. That boy never saw a mirror he didn't look into."

More than once I'd caught him glancing at his reflection in windows and even adjusting the rearview mirror in the car to check out his hair. He did have nice hair. Nice everything.

"You don't have to feel embarrassed," Ella said.

"I'm not embarrassed." There was no point in trying to lie to Ella. "Not much."

"You're not the first person to be dumped."

"That sounds so bad. The dump. Where you put trash or things you don't want. I guess that's how he felt about me. He didn't want me."

"This is harder for you than it would be for most people."

"What does that mean?"

"Come on, Soph, let's not pretend. No one has ever dumped you before."

"I've had breakups."

"And you were always the one who did the breaking up. You were the breaker, not the breakee. Doesn't feel so good from this end, right?"

I knew full well that Ella's last boyfriend had broken her heart. She'd taken it hard. I'd thought she was so negative about Luke because of how badly her relationship had ended. Really, though, she'd just been trying to protect me.

We were friends. She protected me, and I protected her. In the early grades it was mostly me doing the protecting. Ella was wonderful, but she was, well, different, and that didn't play out so well sometimes in middle school. High school could be mean, but middle school was meaner—especially for people like Ella, who said exactly what she was thinking without really thinking it through. She was getting better about that, but blurting was still part of her.

I carefully looked both ways before I eased out of the parking lot and onto the road.

"You've been insulated from some of this breakup stuff because you're so beautiful," Ella said.

"I'm not beautiful."

"Yeah right."

"Well, you're beautiful too."

"No I'm not."

"Yes you are! Don't ever put yourself down like that!" I protested.

"I'm not putting myself down. Luke isn't the only one who looks in mirrors. I know exactly what I look like. I'm cute, perky and, on a good day, in the right light with the right makeup, actually *very* pretty."

"That's right. You're *very* pretty."

"Wait. A few minutes ago you thought I was beautiful," she said.

"I, um, of course you're—"

"Because pretty, even very pretty, is a major step down from beautiful," she said. "From *you*."

My mind spun, struggling for something to say.

"Soph, I know how people, males, react to me and how they react to you. When I'm by myself I get my share of looks. When we're together I'm prepared to be a little less visible."

"I don't even know what that means," I said.

"The guys are all looking at you so hard, they don't notice that I'm there."

"That's not what happens."

"It's the truth, and I'm okay with that." She laughed. "I guess I have to be. You're my best friend, and it's not like you can help it that you're gorgeous. That's probably part of the reason Luke waited until school was over to break it off."

"He said he didn't want to distract me from my exams."

She laughed. "That would be considerate, and he's not. He knew that if you two broke up while school was still on that you'd have won the break-up."

"Nobody wins in those things."

"Of course they do. The first person to be with somebody else after a breakup wins. Even one of his close friends would have chosen you over him. You always win."

"Not always."

"No, always. You always have somebody—and fast," Ella said.

"That almost sounds like an accusation."

"Not an accusation as much as a fact. We've been friends since the seventh grade. How many days were you without a boyfriend or a boy you knew you could have as your boyfriend anytime you wanted?"

I was going to say something, but again there was no point in lying to somebody who knew all my secrets—even the ones I didn't know myself.

"That's what you need to do differently this time," Ella said. "Stay without a boyfriend for a while. It would be good for your soul."

"You make it sound like a religious experience."

"Maybe it is. Think of it as doing meditation or becoming a Buddhist."

"I think Buddhists can date."

"There are hundreds of millions of them, so I assume they do much more than just date," Ella said. "But it would be a real Zen experience for you to be single for a while. Don't be so desperate."

"I'm not desperate."

"It's like you think people will think bad things about you if you don't have a boyfriend."

"I didn't know you thought I was that shallow," I said.

"You're one of the deepest people I know. In fact, your problem is that you overthink everything. It's no secret that you have trouble being spontaneous."

"So you think I'm too predictable."

"You're *very* predictable," she said.

My head tingled. First Luke and then her.

I turned into the parking lot and pulled into a spot beside the ice-cream store. "Luke said I was too predictable. He said I was boring, that I acted too old."

I expected Ella to defend me. She didn't.

"Soph, you know you're my best friend. You know I love you."

"And the *but* in this sentence is...?"

She continued to look at me, as if arranging her words and gathering the courage to say them. It had to be serious for Ella to be thinking before speaking.

"You are very, very, very responsible," she began.

"And that's a bad thing?"

"Sometimes it's a very good thing. You're always the designated driver, the person parents are happy that somebody is going someplace with because they know you'll take care of things. But it's not just that you're like a big sister or even a mother. It's like you're my old-maiden aunt."

For the second time that day, I felt like I'd been kicked in the stomach.

"I'm not saying this to hurt you."

"Then I guess you didn't succeed, because you *did* hurt me."

I climbed out of the car, and Ella jumped out and came after me. "Let me explain!" she called out.

"I think we've talked enough. Let's just get some ice cream."

I reached for the door of the store, and she grabbed me and spun me around. "Soph, I'm sorry if I hurt you. I just thought we were good enough friends for me to be honest."

"I've had too much honesty today. I didn't know my taking care of people was such a problem."

"It isn't. It's one of the things that makes you such a special person." She paused. "It's just that you always want to do the responsible thing, the right thing, the—"

"The boring thing," I said.

"I wasn't going to use that word," she said. "I was going to say the safe thing."

Safe and *boring* sounded like the same thing to me.

"Come on, let's get ice cream. It will make everything better," she said as she pulled open the door and ushered me inside.

I doubted that ice cream could make it better. It was bad enough to be dumped by my boyfriend for being boring, and worse to find out my best friend thought of me the same way.

"And what can I get for you girls today?" the man behind the counter asked.

"I'm thinking," Ella said. "So many choices."

"While she's thinking, I'd like a single scoop of chocolate on a—"

"No she doesn't!" Ella exclaimed.

"Yes I do. You know how I always get chocolate—"

"Yeah, on a waffle cone. Everybody in the world who knows you knows that. Today you don't want chocolate."

"But—"

"No buts. Chocolate is what vanilla people order when they're too chicken to even *admit* that they're vanilla people."

"What are you talking about?" I asked.

"I'm right." She turned to the man behind the counter. "You know I'm right, don't you?"

"She has a point."

"Maybe I just like chocolate."

"More than *every* other flavor?" Ella asked. "More than every other flavor you've never tried? You know the guy has thirty-one flavors, right?"

"Plus we have sherbet," he added.

"I like chocolate."

Ella pointed at the tubs of ice cream. "More than Baseball Nut ice cream? More than Cherries Jubilee or Caramel Turtle Truffle? More than the Amazing Spider-Man ice cream—it even has the word *amazing* in its name. Do you like chocolate more than Candy Corn?"

"That sounds disgusting."

She shrugged. "That does sound disgusting, but how about the classics, like Pralines 'n' Cream or Rocky Road?"

"Isn't chocolate a classic?" I turned to the man for his opinion.

"I guess in that case you should just have vanilla. It is *the* classic and really boring."

Great, I was being ganged up on by the guy selling ice cream. Maybe Ella should text Luke and ask him to come here as well.

"What have you got to lose by trying another flavor?" Ella asked.

"She's right," the man added.

"You have nothing to lose except predictability. Well?" Ella asked.

"I'm not even sure what I should have," I said.

"It doesn't matter as long as it isn't chocolate," Ella said. "Or something like, well, chocolate chip or German chocolate or mint chocolate. It's time for something completely different."

"Tell you what, ladies. This one is on me. No charge. What will it be?" he asked.

I looked at the flavors. There were so many choices—and then I saw what I had to try. I pointed.

The man laughed, and Ella clapped. "One triple scoop of Wild 'n' Reckless sherbet coming up."

DAY 2

"Sophie, get up!"

I opened one eye. Ella was towering over me, standing on my bed.

"What time is it?" I asked sleepily.

"Nine thirty. You slept in. It's time to get up!"

Ella started jumping on the bed, giggling and laughing, going higher and higher, her head almost hitting the overhead fan. Then she bounced off the side and hit the floor with a thud.

"Are you all right?" I struggled to get out of the bed, my feet tangled up in the sheets, and I practically tumbled on top of her before I kicked myself free.

"Better than just all right," she said as I helped her to her feet. "It's the first day of summer break, and there's so much to do. It's going to be a fun summer."

"There'll be time for fun, but I have some work to do as well."

"Did you get a job that I don't know about?"

"Not a job, but I got the reading list for my courses in the fall semester, and I'm going to have most of them read before school starts."

Ella screamed—long and loud.

"I take it you don't approve of my plan."

"It's a simply terrible, *terrible* plan. Maybe the worst plan in the history of the world."

"The worst plan, really?"

"Okay, overly dramatic, I admit. What if I had a better plan for you?"

"Eating ice cream, going to the beach and hanging out isn't really a plan, if that's what you're going to suggest."

"Actually that's a very *good* plan, but I have an even better one than that."

"I'm listening." I'd listen, but doing it was another thing.

"First things first. Breakfast is waiting," she said.

"You made me breakfast?"

"Your father and Oliver made you breakfast."

"Yeah right, my father and brother made me breakfast."

"They did. It's waiting for you," she said.

"But neither of them knows how to cook."

"It's breakfast, not cooking. Come on, or it'll get cold."

"I'll be down in a minute," I said.

She left. I had to do a couple of things first. I quickly made my bed, making sure the pillows were properly positioned and then placed my bear—Snowball—against the pillows. It was wrong not to make your bed when you got up—something neither my father nor brother seemed to get. I headed downstairs.

Before I reached the kitchen I could hear them. My father was laughing and my brother was yelling, and I knew Ella was probably responsible for both. My father and brother liked Ella a lot. In fact, I was pretty sure my brother liked her more than he liked me.

The three of them were on stools around the counter. "Wow." The table was completely laid out—toast, juice, a big pot of coffee, sausages and pancakes.

"You made sausages and pancakes?" I asked my father.

"We made three types of pancakes," my father said. "And good morning to you."

"Um…good morning."

I gave my father a hug. At eleven Oliver was far too old to be hugged by his sister, so I only did that when I wanted to bug him.

"There are blueberry, chocolate-chip and peach pancakes," Oliver said.

I saw three piles of irregularly shaped pancakes. "They look, um, good."

"Don't judge them by their appearance," my father said. "Come, sit down."

"Sorry I slept in. For some reason my alarm didn't go off."

"I turned your alarm off," my father said.

"What?"

"I figured it would be easier to fix breakfast if I didn't have to fight you for the spatula."

My brother got up and started putting things on my plate.

"Okay, what's happening here?" I asked.

"Can't I just be kind to my big sister?" Oliver asked.

"You could, but that's not likely. Again, what's happening here?"

"We just figured that we sort of owe you a breakfast or two," my brother said.

"Or two thousand," my father added.

The math was probably about right. Ever since my mother had died—ever since she'd gotten sick—I'd made breakfast for everybody almost every weekend and on some weekdays. And to add to that, I often made lunch and basically any dinner that wasn't takeout, ordered in or eaten out.

"We thought it would be a nice thing to do before we head off and leave you alone," my father said.

"Your father just told me that he and your brother will be going to your aunt's place to visit for a few weeks," Ella said.

"Oh, didn't I mention that to you?" I asked.

Of course I hadn't. Telling Ella I would have the house to myself for three weeks was a recipe for disaster.

"You're still more than welcome to come with us to your aunt's," my father added.

"I thought it was just going to be the two of us and we were going to be doing some guy stuff," my brother protested.

"Don't worry—I'm still not going. I just want to stay here and relax, do some reading. Besides, somebody has to stay here and take care of the house."

"How responsible," Ella said.

I knew from the tone of her voice she might have said *responsible*, but she was thinking *predictable* or *boring* or *old*.

"Don't worry about Soph when you're gone," Ella said. "I'll be around to take care of her. In fact, I have some plans." She looked directly at me. "We'll talk."

"I told one of my co-workers I was leaving my eighteen-year-old daughter home alone for a few weeks and he thought I was crazy," my father said. "I told him you were more responsible than almost all the adults I know."

Responsible. There it was again. Had my father and Ella talked about me being too responsible? I took a bite of the pancakes. "These are pretty good." I'd worked at ignoring the pieces of eggshell that had found their way into the mix.

"Don't sound so surprised. I do know how to cook," my father said. "Even if you don't let me do it very often."

"*Let* you?" I said.

"I thought I better get back in the habit, with you going off to college."

"I just assumed you and Oliver would be getting takeout every night."

"That's what *I* was hoping for," Oliver said.

I got up, taking my plate.

"We'll take care of that too," my father said as he got up and took it from me. "We have to learn to get by without you. It's not like we're expecting you to come home from college each night to do the dishes. Right?"

"Right," I agreed.

I'd talked to my father about going to the local college so I could stay at home. I'd thought he'd be happy. Instead he got angry. I'd hardly ever seen him so angry. He'd told me that it was my decision to make—to turn down a full scholarship at a prestigious college—but he wasn't going to let me live at home, so I might as well go away to school.

I'd known he was right, that I needed to go away, but still, how would they get along without me? I guessed that's what they were trying to show me right now. It would take a lot more than a few pancakes filled with bits of eggshell to do that.

"In fact, Oliver and I have something to announce," my father said. "Sophie, we know you're worried about us taking care of ourselves. So we've decided that starting now, you are not allowed to make us a meal, do work around the house or care for Oliver."

"You want me to do nothing?" I asked.

"Nothing. We'll take care of ourselves," my father said.

"Do you know how hard that's going to be?"

"We can handle it," my father said.

"And you're agreeing to do that much more work?" I asked Oliver.

"I'll agree to almost anything that includes you not telling me what to do. You're awfully bossy."

"Soph, we just want to show you that we're not helpless," my father added.

"I never thought you were helpless." Fragile, yes, I thought, but kept my mouth closed.

"So Sophie suddenly has lots of free time this summer," Ella said.

"I've still got things to do," I warned.

"But you have lots and lots of free time that you didn't even see coming," Ella said. "I think I might know how to fill that time."

I felt nervous. Very nervous.

❖ ❖ ❖

Ella and I returned to my room while my father and brother cleaned up after breakfast.

"Do you believe that sometimes the stars just align themselves in the right way?" Ella asked.

"Are you asking if I believe in astronomy or astrology?"

"Don't you think it's an amazing coincidence? You and Luke being through and you being freed of all motherly tasks for the summer happening at the same time as I have a plan?"

"What exactly is your plan?"

"You have *no* idea where this is going, and that's why it needs to happen *so* badly."

"That makes no sense, you realize," I said.

"It makes perfect sense. It's cosmic, karmic, hand-of-God stuff."

"Now you're just making me more nervous."

"That's because you need to be in control and know what's happening all the time."

"So now I'm a control freak too," I said.

"Not a control freak, but you are a fish that swims in a sea of predictability."

"Until yesterday I'd never thought predictability was such a bad word," I said.

"With you it *is* a bad word. It's your way of playing it safe. As part of my plan you have to agree to avoid predictability and, more important, be willing to relinquish control."

"I don't need to be in control—I just need to know that things are controlled by somebody."

"And that somebody will be me," Ella said. "Do you trust me?"

"Of course I trust you," I said hesitantly.

"Your words said yes, but your tone said no. Before I go any further, what did you think of your Wild 'n' Reckless sherbet?"

"It was okay." I almost said *almost as good as the chocolate* but didn't.

"I'm glad you liked it, but even if you didn't, it was exactly the prescription you required."

"It was a scoop of sherbet, not medicine."

"It was both. Change is good. New is good. Adventure is good."

"I don't think eating a different type of dessert can be classified as adventure," I said.

"For you it practically is. At least it's the start of an adventure—or a series of adventures." She paused. "There are ninety days between the end of high school and the start of college. That's ninety chances to do something different."

"I don't think there are that many flavors of ice cream or sherbet available," I joked.

"There are actually hundreds of flavors, but this isn't about ice cream or sherbet. I want you to do lots of other different things this summer."

"What kind of different?"

"All kinds of different."

"I'm afraid I'm too *predictable* and *boring* to ever come up with a summer full of new things."

"Please leave sarcasm to an expert. Besides—and this is the truly beautiful thing—I will arrange everything for you. All you have to do is show up."

"And what do you have in mind?"

"I can't really tell you."

"Why not?"

"Partly because it's going to be a surprise and partly because I have no idea yet what things I'm going to arrange.

I want you to think of this as the Surprise Summer of Sophie."

"It does have alliteration. I'll give you that much."

"You also have to give me your word you'll do what I arrange."

"And why exactly should I do this?" I asked.

"First off, it's going to be fun, hilarious, amazing."

"And unpredictable," I practically whispered.

"Yes! Unpredictable and completely out of your control. Soph, how are you feeling about going away to college?"

"Great. Well, good...well, a bit nervous, a little anxious, sort of hesitant, maybe a little uneasy, but that's mainly, you know, about leaving my brother and father alone."

"You know that you're going to do wonderfully, that you'll get great marks. You're scared about it because it's different."

"I'm not really scared."

"Then we'll go with nervous, anxious, hesitant and uneasy. Do all those words work?"

I nodded. All of them, including at least a little scared, fit.

"You're always nervous about *anything* new because you can't control it and you can't predict it. This summer is going to be about unpredictable, out of control. Change is like everything else—the more you do something, the better you get at it. So what do you think?"

I wanted to say no. I wanted to chase Ella from my room and jump back into my perfectly made bed and pull the blankets over my head, but I knew she was right.

"Deal," I said, reaching out my hand to shake on it.

"Just to be clear," she said. "You'll do whatever I arrange for the next eighty-nine days, right?"

"Right."

"No argument, no refusing to do it and you'll go along with whatever I arrange?"

I really wanted to think more about this, but that was so predictable. I just had to do it. "Agreed."

"Then we *do* have a deal."

Instead of shaking my hand, she jumped up and gave me a gigantic hug, almost knocking me off my feet. What had I just agreed to?

"So what's my different thing for today?"

"Don't sound so ominous. It's going to be easy. We're going to sign you up for lots of social media."

"You know I hate all those things."

"And you know you're the only person on the planet under the age of ninety-five who doesn't use social."

"I have Facebook."

"Sophie Evans!" She said, annoyed. "You have an account, but when was the last time you posted anything?"

"A while ago." It had been months and months.

"Through social you're going to share the new and different you with the rest of the world."

"What if I don't want to share?"

"Why wouldn't you? Besides, I know at least one person who needs to know that you're doing all sorts of amazing things."

"I don't care what Luke thinks," I said.

"I didn't even mention his name, so you know you do care," Ella said. "Besides, it's like a tree falling in the forest. If nobody is there to hear it, does it make a noise?"

"Of course it does."

"I'm just making sure that everybody can see and hear the trees fall as you do all those different things! Let's get started by getting you more active on Facebook," Ella said. "It's like you've managed to say absolutely nothing about yourself. Open your page."

I struggled a little because I couldn't remember my password right away.

"I see you have twenty-three friends. There must be monks who've taken a vow of silence and hermits living in caves who have more friends than that."

"I do have some requests, but I just haven't bothered accepting them."

"It's time to accept those requests. By the end of the summer I want you to have thousands of friends," Ella said.

"In real life nobody has thousands of friends."

"Nobody said this was going to be real life. You don't even have an updated picture of yourself. When was this one taken, three years ago?"

"About that. Shouldn't anybody who's truly my friend know what I look like right now?" I asked.

"Again. This isn't real life. We'll put up a picture of you looking really hot—like we could find one where you *didn't* look hot."

There was something about her tone that was, well, almost an accusation.

"A hot picture is a great way to attract new friends," she said.

"It sounds like a great way to attract stalkers."

"Stalkers, lurkers, strangers, people you don't know—all count as friends. We need to get that number up so you don't look like the loneliest person in the world. We also need to update your profile to make you seem more exciting and interesting."

"As opposed to boring and predictable."

"Glad you understand. How about this for a status update?" She started typing.

"*Searching for different*?" I asked.

"That line is important. Which reminds me—we need to change your relationship status," Ella said. With a couple of keystrokes she changed *In a Relationship* to *Single*.

There it was for the world to see.

"Now, what do you think about Twitter?" Ella asked.

"I think Twitter is stupid. Who cares what I had for breakfast?"

"We're not going to tweet about your breakfast. You're going to do some things that people will be interested in."

"I just don't see how I'm going to do that in 140 characters."

"Those characters can include links, and you can post pictures and gifs. You know a picture is worth a thousand words, which is like five thousand characters, if you think about it," Ella explained.

"It sounds like you've been thinking about it enough for both of us."

"And you have to start an Instagram account."

"If Twitter and Instagram both have pictures, why do I need both?"

"Because Insta only has pictures, so you'll get different followers. Plus you'll get likes on your photos, so you get instant gratification."

"And that matters...why?"

"Doesn't everybody like being liked?" Ella asked.

"Pretty well. So is that it?"

"Of course not. You're going to find all of this stuff addictive."

"Is becoming an addict one of the different things I'm going to do?"

"You're already addicted to boring, and you're going to stop cold turkey. You will get a regular injection of excitement as an antidote."

"How can I find the time to do anything different when I'm going to be so busy tweeting, Facebooking and Instagramming?"

"And blogging. You're going to do a blog. We're going to make sure that every tree you fell is going to be heard by lots of people."

"Do I really need everything?"

Ella laughed. "You really don't have anywhere near everything. I could put you on Snapchat, Tumblr, Kik and whatever else is being developed in a garage or basement by some fourteen-year-old boy who has time on his hands because he can't talk to girls."

She sat down at my computer and got to work.

DAY 3

Since the day before, I'd gone from having practically no web presence to what I considered massive social media and learning how to use it. I'd already tweeted, posted pictures, blogged, published and connected. I, or @SophieEvans90, now had seven followers on Twitter and four on Instagram, seven retweets and fifty-seven new friends on Facebook, most of those from accepting pending friend requests that I'd ignored or hadn't really known about.

It was bizarre to be contacted by complete and utter strangers. I had been retweeted in two different countries and favorited in one. How did some guy in New Zealand find out about me, follow me, retweet and like my tweet? It wasn't even that it was such a great tweet—**Follow my journey as I try to do different things for the next ninety days!**

Ella said it probably had more to do with my picture than anything I was tweeting. It was a nice picture. I almost always took a good picture. I wasn't stupid. I knew what I looked like, but I was more than that. I was smart. I was a good student. I tried to always treat people well—even people who didn't necessarily deserve to be treated nicely. I helped people. I was kind.

One of my new Facebook friends was my father—which seemed a little strange. Even stranger, another new "friend" was Luke. I accepted my father's request reluctantly, and Luke's accidentally. His request had been pending for almost a year, and I'd accepted all the pending ones at once. Then I figured it would make me look angry and bitter if I unfriended him a few seconds later. Actually, I *was* angry and more than a little bitter, but he didn't need to know that. I didn't want to give him that satisfaction. It was a shame there wasn't a category called Really Not a Friend But a Stupid Jerk. I would have put him there.

There was another reason not to unfriend him. Ella was right—I wanted him to see that he was wrong about me. Knowing that he would be watching my posts might give me more incentive to do things I really didn't want to do. I knew Ella well enough to know that some of what she was going to suggest or arrange would be more than just uncomfortable.

The hardest part was that I found myself thinking about Luke more than I should—more than I had when we were going out. He was out of my life. But I just couldn't get him out of my head. Was he thinking of me or—I couldn't allow myself to think like that, but how did you stop yourself from thinking? That was something I'd never been good at. There was so much to think about.

Now I had to put up a blog entry about today's different. I wondered what Luke would think about me eating at a place I'd never go with him, and caring what he thought bothered me more than anything.

Today I ate in a Japanese restaurant for the first time. There was an all-you-can-eat restaurant, so I could try anything I wanted. Normally, I wouldn't have wanted anything. Today I had everything—miso soup, California and dynamite rolls, beef teriyaki, vegetable tempura, salmon and tuna sushi and even shrimp sashimi.

Okay, I'll admit I'd heard there could be problems with eating food that isn't cooked—you could get sick or get worms or something. I looked it up and found out that that's hardly ever happened. In fact, it happens less than when people eat food that's cooked wrong.

Some of what I ate was really good, especially some of the rolls and the teriyaki – which of course is actually cooked. The sushi and especially the sashimi were harder to put in my mouth—you have to know that I even like my steak burned. I've always thought that fire and eating utensils were invented so we don't have to eat raw food and use chopsticks. In fact, I still think a fork or spoon works way better than two pieces of wood awkwardly pressed together, but I used them as best I could—and I ate the raw stuff. It was, all in all, pretty good.

Will I eat Japanese again? Yes. Tomorrow? No.

I have the strangest urge to find out what Japanese food would taste like in Tokyo. Of course in Japan they'd probably just call it food! Someday I might find out. For now, sayonara and out.

DAY 5

It had been a long day, and I was feeling tired. At least part of that was because of the adrenaline that was still pumping through my veins. It made me wish I could have just eaten some other type of strange food today. No food would have worked well with today's different, except maybe dry cereal.

I'd already done a status update on Facebook. It was time to put a much longer description about my different up on my blog.

I know that it's called an "amusement" park, not a "terrifying" park, because most people find it amusing. And I do find some things amusing. Waterparks are nice. The Lazy River is a good place to drift for a while. Shows where people sing and dance are good, even when the singing and dancing isn't that good. I like costumed characters who wander around. What I've never liked are the rides. Actually, merry-go-rounds are fun. I'm talking about the rides that jerk you around and around, and the ones that take you high and plunge you down, and the ones that spin you up high. Of all of them, the one I hate to even think about is the one that takes you up high, spins you around, plunges you down, jerks you around and doesn't even let you sit down. I'm talking about the stand-up roller coaster. The only thing that could make it worse is if it had snakes.

Sure, I know that every twelve-year-old and even the really tall nine-year-old who is "must be this tall to ride" goes on it. I've seen them come off laughing and talking, and I know if they can go on it, then I can too. I never wanted to.

Having a friend like Ella, who knows you even better than you know yourself, is a wonderful and dangerous thing. She knows I hate roller coasters. She drove me to today's different. She didn't tell me where we were going until we turned into the park. Then I knew.

The line for the ride was long. Apparently, many people wanted to do this or were being forced to by their best friends. It felt like I was waiting in line to be executed. Or for the dentist. Or for the dentist to execute me.

The moment I was strapped in felt more like the execution and less like the dentist. I wish I could say that was the worst moment, but there were lots of worst moments. The long, slow ride up to the top of the first peak was an exercise in torture. The click, click, click of the machinery, knowing that I had to get higher before I could get lower, wondering if that bored-looking attendant who strapped me in had done it right. There was that moment when we reached the very top—time seemed to stand still—and then we plunged to the bottom.

Lots of people screamed. Some in joy or delight, some in fear. I didn't scream. I couldn't get a sound to come out. The coaster camera caught my expression—terror is the only word to describe it—but you can see for yourself. Ella bought the picture, and I've posted it on both Twitter and Instagram. And then, as the coaster jerked to the side, the movement jarred my lungs enough to release a scream—so long and loud and shrill that it even shocked me. At that same instant I dug my fingers into Ella's hand—we'd been holding hands since we got on—and I figured that even if my harness popped open, I'd hang on to her so hard that either she'd hold me in place or I'd take her off with me. Two of us dying didn't seem so lonely. Besides, since this was all her doing, if I was going to die it seemed only fair we die together!

Finally the ride ended. My knees were weak and my stomach even weaker, but there was this strange sense of joy. No, not joy, exhilaration. I was alive. Then Ella asked me if I wanted to go and do it again. I am proud to report that I didn't hit her.

I took my hands off the keyboard and thought about what should come next. I knew why I didn't like roller coasters and things like that, but did I have to put it out on my blog for everybody else to know? Maybe I did. I started typing again.

I guess it's safe to say that I like to be in control. I used to joke that I'd ride on one of those things if they let me drive. That's not really the case. Lots of highs and lows are beyond anything you can control even if you think you're in control and even if you think you're driving. All you can do is try your best to enjoy the ride or, in some cases, survive the parts you don't want to be there for. Once you start you've just got to hang in there until the finish. I rode the stand-up roller coaster and I won! Another different done.

DAY 6

I looked at my unmade bed. A pillow was on the floor. The cover was all crumpled up at the foot of the bed, the top sheet was balled up, and the fitted sheet had come off one of the bottom corners. I really wanted to straighten it. I placed Snowball—my teddy bear—on the remaining pillow. Just because I couldn't make the bed didn't mean I couldn't make Snowball comfortable. That was my different for the day. I wasn't allowed to make my bed. It had to stay like this all day long.

When Ella had told me this, I'd thought, How stupid. How different is that? Had she already run out of ideas? Big deal—so I couldn't make my bed. How hard could that be? How different was it really?

Instead I found out it was hard, and it *was* different. At least for me.

For as long as I could remember, I'd started the day by making my bed. Today I didn't. I walked away, but I couldn't leave it behind. It was like a little itch I couldn't scratch. When I had to go back into my room throughout the day, it was there, looking at me, smirking at me. Snowball looked confused. Or at least disappointed. It was my bed, but it was her world. And as the day went on, it bothered me how much it bothered me.

I decided I wasn't going to post, publish, tweet or blog about it. There was nothing that interesting about an unmade bed. Nothing interesting, just revealing, and there were some things I didn't want to reveal. Not to the world and a bunch of strangers and lurkers and stalkers. I didn't want to have Luke read about it and chuckle to his friends about how he'd done the right thing.

I looked over at the clock. Only one minute to midnight… and then the clock clicked over. It was midnight. It was the next day. I'd gone the whole day without making my bed. I'd completed the different, and now I could go to bed. I was washed up, makeup off, and in my pjs. That was my every-night routine. But tonight there was still one more thing to do.

I picked up the pillow on the floor and put it in place beside the other. I straightened the bottom sheet and tucked the corners in. I unballed the top sheet and spread it out nicely. I put the cover in place, straightening and flattening until it was perfect. Finally I put Snowball in her place. She looked happy, like she was proud of me. The bed looked so good. It felt so good.

I pulled back the cover and sheet and climbed in. It was cool and soft and perfect, and I felt my whole body relax. I hadn't realized how much the unmade bed had made me feel off until I felt on again.

Right then I decided two things.

"Me having trouble not making my bed is going to be a secret just between you and me," I said to my bear. "You have to promise you won't tell anybody."

Snowball kept silent. It was her specialty.

"It's just sort of embarrassing that it bothered me this much," I added.

The bear looked thoughtful.

"There's one other thing," I said. "I really, really, need this. If an unmade bed bothered me this much, I *need* to do different things. I need to do roller coasters. I need to leave my bed unmade. I just hope Ella can keep on coming up with ideas." I paused. This was the hard part, the part that worried me the most. "And I hope I can be brave enough keep on doing them."

DAY 7

"Are you sure you don't want some?" my father asked.

"I'm not that hungry," I said.

"It's pretty good," Oliver said. "It's homestyle chunky, meaty stew. It's new and improved."

There certainly were chunks, but I wasn't sure if anything else was true. From the second my father had opened the can and the contents made a sucking sound as they were dumped into a pot, I'd known there was nothing in this meal that I wanted.

"I'll pass, thanks."

"Just more for me," Oliver said.

"I feel bad," my father said. "I'm supposed to be fixing meals for you."

"Really, it's more about you two taking care of *yourselves*, not you taking care of me."

He looked guilty. And really, he should have been feeling at least a little guilty. In some ways he wasn't really keeping his commitment to provide for the two of them. Canned stew wasn't cooking. It was hardly food.

"The salad is good, though, right?" he asked.

"Definitely," I said. "Could you pass me the bag?"

Serving food from cans and bags just didn't seem right, but I couldn't say anything more without making my father feel worse.

Oliver handed me the bag of salad. "You can have my share of the salad if you want."

"It's good salad," I said. "It's well-prepared, washed, precut salad."

I wasn't sure who I was trying to convince. I was grateful my father had picked it up at the grocery store. So far over the past few days, I hadn't seen many greens in their diets. I was starting to be afraid that when I went away the two of them would die of scurvy.

We had divided our groceries. I told them it was more realistic for them to prepare to just feed the two of them since I'd be gone, but my father still insisted on trying to feed me some of the time. My food was in the fridge downstairs. That fridge held the remains of an incredible strawberry and pecan salad I'd made the day before. It wasn't even the same species of food as this bagged salad. I'd have some of my salad later on.

It had quickly become apparent that my father hadn't magically acquired the ability to cook. When he'd said he could cook, he meant he could reheat things that came from a can or the freezer. Everything else they'd eaten had been takeout, ordered in or from behind the deli counter at the supermarket.

I really wanted to talk to him about their choices, but I couldn't. That's what mothers said to children, not what daughters said to their fathers. I had to just sit back and wait and hope that their diet improved. There was a learning curve, and he would get better at cooking as he did it more often. It wasn't realistic to expect him to be perfect. Perfection was pretty hard to achieve. I knew that from years of trying.

"So does Ella have something planned for you for later today?" my father asked.

"I don't know. Sometimes she just springs it on me."

"The roller coaster wasn't too bad," he said.

"Only my sister would find it bad to do what everybody else in the world pays money and waits in long lines to do," said Oliver.

"Maybe you should think of it like the stew," I said. "If there were more people like me who hated roller coasters, the lines would be shorter and you could ride more often."

"That makes sense," Oliver said. "I *love* that picture of you and Ella."

He meant the one taken by an automatic camera at the ride. Ella had convinced me, against my will, to put it on Twitter and Instagram.

"Until I saw that picture I would have sworn I'd never seen a bad picture of you," my father said.

"I don't think those sorts of pictures are ever flattering."

"Ella looks okay," Oliver said.

"You just think that because of your future marital plans," I joked.

"Shut up, Sophie."

Ella always kidded Oliver that he was her back-up plan if she didn't find somebody to marry. He told her she was *his* back-up plan if there was no other life on the planet. He protested, but I knew he really did like Ella and was secretly flattered by the attention.

"It's going to be so wonderful to have her as my sister-in-law," I said, trying to agitate him a little bit more.

"Again, shut up, Sophie." He paused. "But she really does look a lot better than you do in that picture."

"He's right," my father said, and I was a little surprised.

"I just *love* the way your face is all squishy and your eyes are all bugged out and you look sort of like this." Oliver distorted his face and opened his eyes as wide as he could.

"I get the idea. The important thing is that it's done and over," I said.

"The ride may be over, but the picture is forever," Oliver said.

"I can always delete it."

"Even if *you* take it down, it's still on Ella's Facebook page as her profile picture."

"What?"

"It's her profile picture. Didn't you know that?" Oliver asked.

I shook my head.

"You should look."

"I will...I guess."

I finished my salad while Oliver practically licked his plate clean. Maybe I'd been wasting my time cooking for him when all he wanted was canned crap. I excused myself and went to my room.

I looked at Ella's Facebook page. There, front and center as her profile picture, was the photo of the two of us on the roller coaster. I looked awful! And Ella *did* look good.

Then I read the caption. **Me and my almost-always-beautiful friend Soph—talk about a different!**

That was sort of funny. And a little bit mean. Maybe I'd ask her to take it down. No, I couldn't do that. That was too, well, vain. Besides, she'd told me I had to change my profile picture every few days, so I had to assume she did the same.

And then I thought back to what she'd said about how people reacted when the two of us walked into a room. If the two girls from that picture strolled into a room, I knew which one the guys would be interested in. It wouldn't be me. And that bothered me a little—okay, more than a little. Is that how Ella felt being around me?

DAY 9

"That was quite the jump in friends and followers in the last few days," Ella said as we drove along.

I now had 356 friends on Facebook, just under 200 followers on Twitter and 78 on Instagram.

"I guess people like pictures of terrified-looking roller-coaster riders," I said.

"That was some picture of us!" Ella laughed.

She'd kept it as her profile picture, and I'd thought a lot about it the last two days. This was my opening.

"*You* look pretty good."

"I look gorgeous!" Ella said.

"Better than I look."

"I've never seen you look so awful, and that's what makes it so hilarious." She paused and looked at me. "You're not having a problem with that, are you?"

I wanted to blurt out the truth, but I didn't. "It's just a picture."

"Good. I was afraid you were going all prima donna on me."

"Is that how you see me?"

"Not really, although you're certainly more made up today than you usually are."

I shrugged. It was true that I'd taken a little more time with my makeup, and I was wearing a new top. And maybe it did have to do with that bad picture. Did that make me a prima donna?

"And here we are," Ella said as she turned into the parking lot of Burger Barn.

"Aren't we about three hours early for lunch?"

"We are definitely early for lunch, but just on time to report to work. You are one of the Burger Barn's newest employees," Ella said.

"You arranged for me to work at a burger place?"

"Yes, I applied online, and we were both hired. I didn't want to miss out on having or watching the fun. Apparently, they'll just about take anybody, sight unseen. Training starts in ten minutes."

"But how is this a different? I worked in a fast-food place before—two summers ago with you, remember?"

"I've tried hard to blur that memory. I also remember you were such a diligent little worker bee that you were the employee of the week half the time."

"So how is us working here a different?" I asked.

"For starters, the last time you worked fast food, you were trying relentlessly hard to do a good job."

"And this time I'm not?"

"Your mission is to do such a terrible job that you get fired, stripped of your uniform and hairnet, before the end of the lunch rush."

"You *want* me to get fired?"

"Not just fired, but *gloriously* fired. I want them to put your picture on the wall as the *worst* employee of the week, month and year. I want you to become a legendary bad employee. You remember all those stupid things customers said to us, all the ridiculous requests, all the dumb orders given by stupid supervisors?" Ella asked.

"Some of them are hard to forget because they were *magnificently* stupid."

"And do you remember how you just had to suck it up, nod your head, smile and pretend the customer and the boss were always right when they were clearly wrong?"

"That's part of the reason I never wanted to work fast food again."

"Today you will look forward to those comments, enjoy them and *react* to them. Forget about the customer always being right. The customer is going to be painfully, relentlessly, always wrong. Today, instead of being the best employee you can be, you have to be the worst employee imaginable. Do you accept your different?"

"Um...it's just that I'm not sure if I can be a bad employee. You know I like to do my best."

"You will do your best at being bad. Well?"

It might be fun. "I gave you my word, Ella."

"Oh, by the way, you should start calling me Sky."

"What?"

"On the applications, I wrote that I was Sky Fall and you are Meadow Fields."

"That's ridiculous."

"What's ridiculous is that nobody even questioned those names."

"But why didn't you just fill out our real names?"

"Oh, believe me, by the time this is over you're going to be so glad they don't know your real name."

❖ ❖ ❖

The training was pretty easy. Of the five new Burger Barn employees, Ella and I were not only the oldest but the only two with experience. That didn't surprise me. People who had experienced fast-food employment once seldom did it again.

We were dressed in our new uniforms. Well, new to us—mine had a stain at the back. How I would have liked to wash it before putting it on. They were also ill fitting, worn and a strange color combination of mustard, brown and white, which were the official colors of Burger Barn. To top it all off, we wore little badges that read *Trainee—please be patient*. Our plan, of course, was to push people's patience to the breaking point.

We had asked to work at the front, and the manager, Barney, was thrilled to oblige, in part because of our experience but also because nobody else wanted to. It was definitely the hardest and worst place to be, because it required direct contact with customers. Ella had said that's what made it the best place for us to be, and that's what was scary.

Barney said he had himself "a couple of keepers" in the two of us. Boy, was he going to be proven wrong.

We were going to be a pair, me working the cash register and Ella getting the meals. Barney hovered over us as we handled the first few customers. The register was easy, and the menu was simple.

"Meadow, Sky, you are both doing incredibly well," Barney said.

He sounded so proud that it made me feel guilty.

"Thanks," Ella said. "Do new employees qualify for employee of the week?"

"It's employee of the month, and they definitely do," Barney said.

"That's what we're aiming for, right, Meadow?"

I'd almost forgotten my name. "Yes, that's my goal." In real life that always was my goal, whether it was working in a fast-food place or getting the best marks or being the star of the volleyball team.

"I was employee of the month eleven times when I was front line," Barney said. "You know, before I made the big move into management."

"Somehow that doesn't surprise me," Ella said.

It didn't surprise me either, but it did sound a bit pathetic that he was so proud of it. Had I sounded that pathetic or that proud?

"Meadow was often the employee of the week where we used to work."

"Good to know. I suspected as much."

He gave me a big goofy smile. Great, just what I wanted. Ella had been kidding me, saying she thought Barney had a little crush on me.

"Burger Barn has a strong corporate culture that believes in the benefits of promoting from within," Barney said.

"So if we do a good job, we could someday be managers?" Ella asked. I heard the sarcasm, but Barney didn't.

"I like the way you're reaching for the stars," Barney said.

"It's good to have a plan," I said, jumping in before Ella could say anything about him seeing his job as being the stars.

"Let's get through the first shift before you start taking over," Barney said. "I like that type of ambition in my—"

"Barney, we have a problem with the fryer!" another employee said as she rushed up.

"I'll be right there," he said and then turned his attention back to us. "Do you think you two can handle this solo?"

"We won't be solo. We'll take care of each other," Ella said.

"I love that confidence and that sense of teamwork. I'll be back soon," he said and left.

"Game on," Ella said enthusiastically.

"Yeah, game on." I could repeat the words, but I wasn't feeling the same way.

I turned to the customer standing in front of me. "Welcome to Burger Barn. What can I get you today?"

"I'd like a number three meal with extra biggie fries," the man said.

I started to punch in the order, and Ella tapped me on the arm. "Is that it?" she asked. "Don't you have something else to say to the customer?"

This was actually going to happen. I turned back to the man.

"Um...do you know that meal has over two thousand calories?" I asked him.

"Um, no, not really," he mumbled.

"Shouldn't you be having a salad instead?" I suggested. I felt uneasy and guilty saying that.

"What?" he asked.

Ella gave me a little nudge in the back. There was no point in only going partway.

"I think you should have a salad. Obviously, you haven't been having enough of them."

"She's right," Ella said. "I think you've had a few combos too many."

I held my breath, waiting for his reaction.

"Um...maybe you're right," he said.

"What?" I asked.

"Yeah, make it a salad, and hold the dressing," he said. "And give me a water to drink."

I could hardly believe what he'd said. Ella went to get the salad and water. She handed it to him.

"No charge," I said.

"Really?" the man asked.

"It's Free Salad Saturday. You deserve a free meal for making a healthy choice," I said.

"Thanks! Thanks so much!"

He looked like he'd won the lottery. Maybe giving away food wasn't the best way to make people angry.

"Tell your friends that's the new policy at Burger Barn—healthy is free!" Ella yelled out after him.

"That was a spectacularly good start. I really didn't know you had it in you," she said to me.

"Neither did I, but isn't that the plan?" I asked.

"Yeah, but giving away food is a bad start unless the manager hears you do it. Ramp it up—I want to get out of here."

"Next," I barked at the woman in line. "What do you want?"

"I'm not sure...I was thinking that..."

"Time for thinking is over. You've been standing in line. You should have made a decision before you got here. If you don't know what you want, step aside. I don't have time to waste," I said.

"What did you say?" she asked.

"It's Burger Barn, not fine dining. The whole menu is up there on the board," I said, gesturing behind me. "It's not like one of these meals is any better than the other, so just order something."

She looked shocked. I was shocked at how good that felt. Rather than guilt I felt relief and joy at finally saying what I'd been thinking every day of the summer when I'd worked fast food.

"Okay, you've lost your chance," I said. "Step aside, and I'll serve the person behind you."

I braced for her reaction. Was she going to yell or demand to see the manager or—

She compliantly stepped to the side. I heard laughter from Ella but didn't look back.

"You better know what you want," I snapped, pointing my finger at the couple next in line, who were about my age.

"We do!" the girl exclaimed. They'd obviously overheard what I'd said.

"Go ahead."

"We'd like a number one combo and a number three with extra cheese and bacon," the guy said, "and make the drinks Cokes."

"Who's the number three for?" I demanded.

The guy raised his hand.

"Really? You know she's dating down to be with you as it is. Do you really think you can afford to chunk up?"

The girl laughed. "See, it isn't just my girlfriends saying things like that."

I snatched the twenty-dollar bill from his hand as the two of them started to argue.

"Stop fighting or take it outside," I said. "Or at least step to the side."

They continued to argue as I turned to the next person in line. I'd started to take the woman's order when Ella returned with the two meals. Neither drink cup had a lid, and cola sloshed slightly over the edges as she put them down. That gave me an idea. I hit both drinks, and they toppled over, the cola splashing over the counter, people jumping back and screaming. At least it stopped the couple from arguing.

Next I grabbed the triple burger with bacon and cheese and took a gigantic bite out of it, then handed it to the startled guy.

"This is awful!" I called out. "Did they put extra cheese or extra disgusting on this?"

"What? What are you doing, what are you saying?" It was Barney. His eyes were wide, and his expression couldn't have been more confused if I'd taken a bite out of him instead of the burger.

"This burger is disgusting," I yelled. I reached over, grabbed it back from the startled customer and held it out for Barney. "Try it yourself—have a bite." I pushed it into his face, and he stumbled back a step. Shocked didn't describe his reaction. He looked terrified, like he was dealing with a crazy person. Okay, he *was* dealing with a crazy person. Was this really me?

Everyone in the whole restaurant was silent, every sound stopped, every eye on me. Nobody moved—it was like the entire restaurant was frozen in place. I braced, waiting for Barney—or anybody—to react. There was nothing. They all stood stunned, silent and still as statues.

"You know, if staff occasionally washed their hands after using the facilities this food wouldn't taste nearly as bad," I said.

A groan went up from the people, and somebody yelled, "That's disgusting!" Someone else said, "I told you so!" But from Barney there was nothing. I could see the wheels turning, but he was struggling to speak. Instead he just made gurgling sounds, like he had so many words he wanted to say that they were all stuck in his throat. How could he fire me if he couldn't talk?

I grabbed the two cartons of French fries that remained on the tray and tossed them into the air. They rained down on the customers, unfreezing everybody as they exploded in movement and screams and laughter.

"You-you-you," Barney stuttered. "You are-are—"

"Come on, say the word—you can do it," Ella said encouragingly from behind.

"Fired! You are *fired*!" he screamed.

Ella and I screamed out in delight, jumping up and down and hugging as the customers looked on in amazement and disbelief.

⁂

I posted getting fired and then put up a picture of Ella and I dressed in our uniforms and a second one of me knocking over the drinks. Ella had even managed to take a video of me with

Barney, ending with me tossing the fries in the air. We'd put that on YouTube and posted the link on Facebook and Twitter. It had already been viewed by almost three thousand people! It wasn't like a kitten playing a piano, gone viral with millions of views, but still, it was pretty amazing. And, of course, the more people who saw the video, the more followers I got on Twitter and Instagram. In one day I'd gotten almost three hundred friend requests, dozens and dozens of retweets and lots of new followers. It seemed like everybody in the world had not only worked at a fast-food restaurant at one time but had wanted to do exactly what I'd done. In some strange way I had become a fast-food hero. And, as bizarre, this was even better than being employee of the month.

I'd been racing through friend requests, just checking them off, when one caught my attention. It was Barney, the manager of Burger Barn. I accepted his request, and then he put up a nice message thanking me for making him "famous" and saying there were no "hard feelings." He also wanted me to know there had been a "bump" in business at the Burger Barn by people coming in after seeing the video. He invited me back to have lunch—on the house—if I promised not to start a food fight.

Ella had told me she was proud of me and that I'd surprised her with how extreme I'd gotten. I'd surprised myself even more. How many surprises did I did have inside of me still to come?

DAY 11

My blog entry for today:

How stupid for me to write in the roller-coaster blog that I hate snakes.

Ella didn't know that—until she read about my fear. I had gotten a terrible sinking feeling when we pulled up and I read the sign. Reptile World. *Snakes. It had to be snakes.*

I was right. The place was filled with snakes. So many of them, and each one creeped me out. Then we stopped in front of the cage that was home to the one Ella had brought me to "meet." It was the biggest snake I'd ever seen in my life. An anaconda.

Before I could meet it, I met the trainers/owners of the place, a couple called Chip and Amber. Both of them were covered in tattoos—mainly of snakes, which were on their arms and in Chip's case "coiled" around his neck and up onto the side of his face.

I went into the snake pen with them. I was really scared stiff. Amber took my hand and made me gently touch the snake. It felt different than I thought it would. It was warm and soft and smooth. Then they picked the snake up—it took the two of them—and gently draped it around my neck. That's the picture you see—a fifteen-foot anaconda wrapped around my neck. I'm not sure why I'm smiling, but somehow it seemed almost surreal—until I realized I couldn't breathe so well anymore. That's when the pictures stopped and the keepers and photographer and Ella all worked to unwrap it from my neck.

DAY 15

The knot in the pit of my stomach was from a combination of adrenaline and anxiety. What a strange way to feel about going to the shopping mall. I looked around furtively, trying to see what dangers or different could be lurking. There was nothing but stores and shoppers. No heights or snakes or roller coasters.

Ella was all smiles and confidence, but why wouldn't she be? It wasn't like I had something planned for her.

"So what's going to be happening today?" I asked.

"Maybe we're just going for a stroll in the mall. Don't you like the mall?"

"I'm not that big into shopping—you know that."

"Believe me, we're here to shop but not to buy," Ella said.

The knot got tighter. "Can't you just tell me what we're going to be doing?"

"It's not *we*, it's *you*, and I'll tell you soon enough. You have to admit that I've arranged some pretty interesting things for you to do so far."

"I'm not arguing with that." They *had* been interesting, but she really seemed to enjoy watching me twist in the wind.

"And let's be honest. These aren't the things you'd normally do."

"These are things that no normal person would normally do," I said.

"Normal people go on roller coasters and eat sushi and sherbet."

"Normal people don't try to get fired from a job at Burger Barn."

"Normal people don't want to work at Burger Barn to begin with. Getting fired was simply a part of pushing you. Do you want to stop?"

I thought about that for a split second. Part of me did want to stop. I couldn't let that part win. I couldn't let the unmade bed beat me.

"No. Keep them coming. I can handle different."

"I like that confidence—even if it's false confidence. Part of the reason I don't tell you in advance—besides the fact that it really does amuse me not to—is that I know how you worry."

I did worry. No question. Wait. "Amuses you?"

"It is funny to watch you go through these things." She paused. "Is that mean of me?"

"No, of course not."

"Come on, when you watch *America's Funniest Home Videos*, don't you laugh when people fall down?" Ella asked.

"Of course. A little." But they weren't people I knew.

"You know what they say—it's funny until somebody gets hurt, and then it's hilarious."

"I'll see if I can make things more hilarious for you."

"That's so considerate of you! But there's no chance of you getting hurt today. And as I speak, here we are."

We were in the middle of the food court. It was almost noon, and there were lineups at all the fast-food counters. All the seats were taken, and people were wandering around, trays in hand, waiting for tables to open up.

"And to make it even easier for you," Ella said, "I'm going to give you hundreds of choices."

There were dozens of little food places, but not hundreds. I was confused.

"I thought we'd already done the food thing. This won't be a genuine different."

Ella laughed. "I'm going to let you select from a menu of different types, but food has nothing to do with it. How many people do you think are here?"

There were many, many people here—many, many to witness whatever I was about to do. It would be a very public display, whatever it was. My stomach tightened even more.

"You get to pick a person," Ella said.

"Pick a person for what?"

"To kiss."

"What?" I gasped.

"You know what a kiss is. I want you to walk up to somebody and give them a kiss."

"You want me to kiss a perfect stranger."

"Soph, nobody is perfect, although those guys over there at the table by the KFC look pretty close to it."

I looked. There were three guys about our age having a meal. As I watched them, one of them looked over at us, and we made eye contact. He gave a little smile and a slight nod of his head. The others turned around to look in our direction, and I looked away.

"Ella, get serious. Do you really expect me to just walk up to somebody I don't know and kiss them?"

"Of course not. You can introduce yourself, say a few words—you can even ask for permission if you want."

"What if they say no?"

"Then you find somebody else. I'm sure somebody will kiss you. You'll find some willing participant in our social-science experiment."

"I don't know if I can do this."

"Are you telling me there's not one person in this whole mall you wouldn't want to kiss?" Ella asked.

"Of course there'd be somebody. It's not that. I can't just kiss a stranger."

"First off, once you kiss him he won't be a stranger. Second, it sounds like if you did that, you'd be doing something different, something you've never done. Wait, aren't you *supposed* to be doing something different for ninety days? Look, just take it a step at a time."

"And what exactly is the first step?"

"Select the person you think you'd like to kiss. Just look around. There's no harm in doing that, is there?"

I shrugged. She was right. I looked beyond Ella to the herd that surrounded us. Hundreds and hundreds of people were grazing. The three guys were still there, eating now, mercifully, not looking in our direction. They were cute. It wouldn't be the worst thing to kiss one of them.

"Okay," I said as I started to walk away.

"Okay you'll do it?"

"Okay I'll look around."

I started walking, glancing from table to table and over at the people standing in line to place their orders or get their food.

"See anybody you like?"

"Ssshhhh," I said. "Let me at least look in peace."

I worked my way between the tables. So many people, so many *potential* choices, yet so few *real* choices. There seemed to be a lot of females and older people—many, many senior citizen types and mothers with small children, but not that many people around my age. Then again, I could go for a little bit younger or a lot older. That would increase the number of potential recipients of my kiss.

That sounded so strange, even saying it in my head. I was going to walk up to some stranger and just plant a kiss on him. What if he had the flu or bad breath or something worse? What if he yelled at me for even suggesting it?

"Well, do you see someone?" Ella called.

"I see lots of somebodies but not a specific someone."

"You're being too picky."

"Picky. Do you see somebody you'd just walk up to and kiss?" I asked.

"I see half a dozen, including the three guys I'd already pointed out, but maybe I'm not picky enough. Just make a choice. It's not like you're going to marry him or date him or even see him again. But who knows—you might turn a frog into a prince."

"Only a princess could do that."

"Well then, that might just work today."

Did she mean she thought *I* was a princess? I was going to say something when I spotted the person. He was on the other side of the court, and I couldn't see all of him, but I just knew. It had to be him.

"The sooner you do it, the sooner we can—"

"I found him."

"You did? Where is he, where is he?"

"Right over there," I said and pointed.

"There are a lot of people over there. Which one?"

"You'll just have to wait and see."

Ella wasn't the only one who could play this game.

I walked between the tables, dodging people with trays who were too busy looking for a seat to look out for me. When I stopped, Ella bumped into me from behind. I turned around.

"A little privacy would be nice," I said. "I want *you* to give me a bit of distance."

"But I have to be close enough to take pictures," she argued.

"Your phone camera has a zoom."

Ella looked like she was going to argue, but she didn't. She stayed and I walked.

The closer I got, the more certain I was. The resemblance was uncanny—and I wouldn't have noticed if it wasn't for Ella's bizarre request.

I stopped in front of his table. His head was down, and he was reading a newspaper. There was a coffee cup on the table. I stood there, unsure what to say, thinking I should just leave, and then he looked up. "Hello."

"Hello."

"Do you want the table?" he asked.

"Um, no, but could I join you?"

"What?"

"Could I join you?" I asked louder.

"Of course, but you'll have to speak up. My hearing aid doesn't always work so well when there's so much background noise."

"I understand," I said, speaking even louder.

As I sat, he rose slightly to his feet. "You don't need to do that," I said.

"People of my generation were raised to show courtesy to a female."

I guessed he was somewhere in his late seventies or early eighties. "My grandfather would have done the same thing," I said. "You look like him—a lot."

He laughed. He even laughed like my grandfather. "I think when we get to a certain age, we all start to look alike. How old is your grandfather?"

"He was eighty-one when he passed."

"Sorry to hear that."

"It was a while ago." Almost five years. "But I still miss him."

"That's sweet. I'm pretty close to my grandkids. I just wish we didn't live so far apart. They're on the other end of the country."

"My grandpa didn't live close either."

He was my mother's father, and when he died it felt like losing a little more of her. He'd told me that her dying was the hardest thing he'd ever gone through, and that the only people who truly understood were my brother and father and me, because we'd lost her too.

"He died without me being able to say goodbye to him," I said.

"That's sad for everybody. I'm sure he knew you cared for him."

"He knew. I just wish I could have done one more thing."

"What was that?" he asked.

"Give him a goodbye kiss on the cheek."

"That's so sweet." He paused. "I know I'm not your grandfather, and it's not the same, but if you wanted to..." He turned to the side and with one finger pointed to his cheek.

I got up slightly in my seat, leaned across the table and kissed him on the cheek.

"It's been a few years since a beautiful young woman wanted to kiss me. Although I still get kissed on a regular basis by a woman who isn't quite so young but I think is still beautiful."

"Your wife?"

He nodded. "My wife of fifty-two years. My wonderful Anita. She's here somewhere in the mall. She shops, and I read the paper. It seems to keep us both happy."

"That's lovely."

"I'm probably not going to tell her about this little kiss though. Every marriage needs a little mystery, and I wouldn't want her to be jealous."

"Then I better get going before she comes back."

"Probably best," he said.

I got to my feet. "Thank you."

"No, thank *you*. It was my honor to be your grandfather's stand-in."

I walked over to Ella. I expected her to look annoyed. Instead she was all smiles.

"That wasn't exactly what I had in mind," she said.

"This was better than you had planned. Thank you, Ella, thank you for pushing me a little bit more."

DAY 17

I looked up from my book as Oliver slammed the refrigerator door closed—again. This was his third trip in the last ten minutes, and each time he came away empty-handed. Whatever he was looking for, he hadn't found it, and he wandered out of the kitchen.

I turned back to my book. It was for one of my first-semester courses, and I was having trouble focusing on it. It wasn't necessarily boring, but I was feeling a little distracted. Between the things Ella was arranging and the fact my father and brother were going away tomorrow, my head was too occupied with the present to think much about what was going to happen in September. September was a lot of days and a lot of differents away.

I'd continued to share some meals with my father and brother, but mostly the two of them cooked and shopped separately. Their food was in the main fridge in the kitchen, and I was using a little bar fridge in the rec room that was about the size of the one I would have in my college dorm room. I'd told my father I was getting myself prepared, but that was only part of it.

The sight, the smell, the sucking sound of food exiting the can and plopping onto a plate to be microwaved was more than I could handle. Did anything that plopped ever taste good and could it ever be good for you?

I'd heard a lot about the "freshman fifteen," which supposedly was how many pounds a first-year college student usually put on. There was no way I was going to let that happen to me. I was way too in control to—

Control. That was another one of those bad words, like *responsible* or *predictable.*

Oliver came back into the kitchen and opened the fridge door. He sighed like he'd sprung a leak. "There's nothing in here to eat. We need food."

"What you really need is the fridge food fairy to arrive," I said.

Still holding the door open, he looked at me in confusion. "Fridge fairy?"

"Fridge *food* fairy," I said. "You know. The magical creature who puts food in the fridge every night when everybody in the house is asleep. Isn't that how it works?"

"It always did before."

"Think of this as a magic wand," I said as I held up the pen in my hand. "Just make a list or even call Dad at work and have him bring the food you want home after work."

"After work is a long time from now, and I'm hungry now."

"There must be something to eat in there."

He opened the door wider and stepped aside. There really wasn't much.

"Because we're going to Auntie Janice's place tomorrow, Dad didn't want to leave food that would just go bad."

"How about opening a can of something?"

"I finished up the types I like. I ate the last can of Scary O's for breakfast."

"You had Scary O's for breakfast?" I asked disgustedly.

"It's not just a lunch and dinner thing, you know."

"It's hardly a food thing. What about fruit?" I asked.

"No fruit. We just have some apples."

"Apples *are* fruit."

"Not tasty fruit. *Fruit* is a banana or an orange. A watermelon or even baby carrots."

"Carrots are a vegetable."

"I said, *baby* carrots. The older ones are vegetables. But we don't have any of those anyway."

"Look, I have fruit, and you're welcome to go and take some."

He looked all excited and then hesitant. "I don't think I can do that."

"Why not?"

"You know, it's not our agreement. Dad might get mad at me."

"It's hard to get Dad mad at anybody for anything," I said. "Besides, it's not like I'm fixing you food. I'm just sharing what I have, the way I would with Ella or any of my friends."

"I'm not a friend. I'm your brother."

He closed the fridge door with a loud slam and went over and opened up a cupboard. He pulled out a box of Cheerios.

"I figure if I can have Scary O's for breakfast, I can have Cheerios for lunch."

He pulled out a fistful of cereal. Some dropped onto the floor, and the rest he stuffed it into his mouth.

"Are you going to get a bowl and milk for that?" I asked.

"Bowls we have. Milk we don't. Besides, this way there are no dishes to wash."

He walked out of the kitchen, a few more little O's dropping out of his hand and onto the floor as he went.

Thank goodness they were going to my aunt's for the next few weeks so they could get some good food. But that wasn't going to help them when they came back and when I went away to school. This whole thing was to prove to me that they could get along without me. So far they'd only been proving the opposite.

DAY 19

The car was all packed, and they were ready to leave.

"So what are you forgetting?" I asked my brother.

"I'm not forgetting how much I'm going to enjoy not having you around to not nag me about what I'm forgetting."

"That doesn't even make grammatical sense."

"Not to mention being free of you correcting me for the next three weeks. How are you going to survive without somebody to boss, correct or nag?"

"Somehow I'll survive." Luke had talked, too, about my correcting him. Did I really do it that much?

My father walked up and joined the conversation. "Are you completely sure you don't want to join us?"

"I promised Ella I'd be here for our adventures."

"It's just that it seems wrong for us to go away without you when in September you'll be going away. We're really going to miss you," my father said.

"Speak for yourself!" my brother said.

"I know I'm going to miss you enough for both of us," my father said as he wrapped an arm around me.

He really was a nice, sweet, kind guy. That was part of what made me worry so much about him.

"So do you have everything?" I asked him.

"I hope so, because if I have to put anything else in the car, I'll need to leave your brother at home."

"I'll ride on the roof if I have to," he said.

"I'll help tie you to the roof if I have to," I added.

"Then we better get going," my father said, and the two of them got into the car.

I felt a tinge of sadness. This wasn't an Ella-initiated different, but it *was* a different. This was the first time I hadn't been part of a family trip. I thought back to all those trips, back to the times before Oliver was even born, when it was just my dad and my mother and me, and the feeling of sadness got much stronger all of a sudden.

"Ella's coming over today, right?" my father asked, leaning out the car window.

"She is."

"And does she have something planned for you today?"

"She does, but she won't tell me what it is."

"She knows you'd just worry."

Everybody knew that worry was part of my standard equipment.

"I just want you to know that no matter how wild it sounds, whatever she suggests you do, well—"

"I know. Be careful, and think about it and be safe," I said.

"Actually, I was going to say the opposite. *Don't* be careful, don't be thoughtful, don't be safe. Just do it. Okay?"

"This has to be the strangest goodbye wisdom a parent has ever given their teenager when they're leaving her alone at home for three weeks," I said.

"Maybe that says something significant about you, or me, or our relationship. I can always count on you to be responsible. Maybe this time you have to be at least a little irresponsible, and maybe even a little stupid?"

I laughed. "Yes, I promise to be irresponsible, stupid, uncareful, unthoughtful and unsafe while you're gone."

"That's my girl!"

"I'm pretty sure *uncareful* isn't even a word," Oliver said, leaning across the seat. "Maybe you should have been unresponsible as well."

"I love you, Oliver."

"And we love you," my father said. "We'll see you in three weeks, and you know you can reach us anytime you need to."

"We'll talk. Every day. Count on it."

My father backed out of the driveway, and then he waved. Even my brother waved. And I waved back until they were halfway down the block, watching until they turned the corner and disappeared.

❖ ❖ ❖

The credits rolled at the end of the movie. Thank goodness it was over.

"That was incredible," Ella said.

"Incredibly bad. That plot made no sense whatsoever."

"It's a horror movie. The plot isn't supposed to make sense."

"Yeah, but why did all the characters keep going off by themselves?" I asked. "It was just stupid that they didn't figure out that it meant they were going to die."

"Okay, point taken. Didn't you want to just yell, *Stay together, you idiots, and whatever you do, don't go into the basement*?"

"If they could have heard the creepy background music, they would have known. Really, those were all such seriously stupid people they deserved to be murdered."

"People in horror movies have to continually do the stupidest things possible to keep the plot moving forward, and you'd know that if you'd ever seen one before," Ella said.

"I never wanted to see one before, and I doubt I'm ever going to see one again. I just don't get it. Why do people want to be scared?"

"It might be that they like to feel smarter than the people in the movies. Or maybe it makes them feel alive. You have to admit, for something so predictable you were still surprised sometimes. That shows some cleverness," Ella said.

"Jumping out of a closet wearing a mask would be a shock, but that doesn't mean it would be clever," I said.

Ella looked a little uneasy. I knew why, but she didn't know that I knew.

"Well, I've now seen one horror movie, so I've done my different for the day."

"No argument, and you kept your eyes open for most of it," Ella said.

"Closing my eyes wouldn't have helped. The screaming and chopping and slashing were the worst parts."

"What do you expect from an ax murderer?" she said.

"I still don't get why they just didn't leave the cabin and get away," I said.

"Their cars didn't work because the ax murderer had chopped up the tires and engines, remember?"

"But they could have walked or run away."

"They were deep in the woods. It was too far to walk," Ella said.

"If four of your friends had been viciously hacked to death in a cabin, wouldn't you be prepared to walk really far and really fast?"

"I would have been moving so fast that the only way I would have been caught was if the ax murderer was an Olympic marathon champion. Even then, it would have been kind of like being chased by a bear."

"I don't get it."

"You don't have to outrun the bear. You only have to outrun one of your friends."

"You'd sacrifice me?" I asked.

"In a heartbeat."

I felt a little hurt, and it must have showed.

"Wouldn't you sacrifice me if it came down to the two of us?" she asked.

I didn't answer.

"But realistically, if we were in a horror movie, you'd probably be one of the last ones killed. You might even survive."

I gave her a questioning look.

"You haven't watched any other horror movies or you'd know that the hot girl is almost always the last to be killed or the only one to survive. Spunky, cute best friend almost always gets killed before her."

"Are we going to talk about this again?"

"Do you think one bad picture of you on social has changed that?"

She still had that roller-coaster picture up on Facebook.

"Of course I wouldn't be the first to be killed," she continued. "Usually the annoying guy, then the rich, snobby girl and then the chubby guy are the ones to be sacrificed. You'd definitely know that pattern if you watched a few more of these movies," Ella said.

"Then I guess I'll have to take your word for it, because I'm not planning on ever watching another one."

"Okay, but getting back to that being-chased-by-a-bear thing, are you saying you wouldn't do the same and sacrifice me to save your own life?" she asked.

I shook my head. "I'm way too responsible for that."

"You're right. You probably would have tried to reason with the ax murderer as well, asked him to take off his bloody boots and leave them at the door along with his ax. You would have reasoned with him until he took his own life to get some peace."

"Is that how you feel?" I asked. Is that what Luke felt, that he needed to get away from me to get some peace?

"Of course not." She got up and started to walk away.

"Where are you going?"

"I just want to get something from my bag."

"Something...like this?" I asked. I reached under the couch and pulled out a ghoulish mask featuring the image of the murderer in the movie we'd just watched.

"You went into my bag?"

"Of course I went into your bag."

"That's, that's, well, wrong."

"Would it be as wrong as wearing a mask and jumping out of a closet?" I asked.

"It wasn't going to be a closet." She paused. "It was going to be in your bathroom. You spoiled my surprise."

"Not that much of a surprise. It's not just *you* who thinks she has her best friend all figured out. I know you pretty well too, so I thought there'd be more to this than just the movie."

"Obviously." She turned to continue walking away.

"Where are you going now?" I asked as I jumped to my feet.

"Now I'm just going to the washroom. Are you planning on joining me?"

"I might. If that one girl had taken a friend to the washroom with her, she wouldn't have ended up in hacked pieces stacked in the bathtub."

"At least he was being neat and tidy. I thought you'd respect that part."

Part of me *had* appreciated that part. I followed after her.

"So is your plan now not to be alone at all tonight, even for a second?"

"Not a bad plan."

"Funny, if it was a stupid, unbelievable plot that made no sense whatsoever, what exactly are you afraid of?" Ella asked.

"I think maybe you should get used to having me glued to your side until the morning."

Ella looked at her watch. "I guess I can wait fifteen minutes before I use the facilities."

"Why wait?"

"Because in about five minutes my father is picking me up to go home."

"You're going to your father's tonight?" I gasped. "Why?"

"Because that's where I live at least part of the time."

"I know where you live. I thought you were sleeping over."

"You being alone overnight is another different. If I'm not mistaken, you've never been alone overnight, have you?"

"No. I knew you weren't going to stay over every night while my family is gone, but why tonight, after that movie?"

"This whole horror-movie thing really enhances and heightens the whole different, don't you think? You're lucky I couldn't actually arrange a cabin in the woods," she said.

We heard a car horn honking.

"Perfect timing. That would be my father." Ella gave me a big hug, and I hugged her back—hard.

"Don't worry, you're going to be all right. It was just a movie."

"I know, I know."

She grabbed her bag, and I followed her to the door.

"If you're really that scared, I could stay," she said.

"Don't be silly. Your father came all this way to get you."

"You're sure?"

"I'm sure. I'll be fine."

"If you need to, you can call me. Anytime during the night, if you need to. I'll leave my phone on."

"I'm going to be all right. I'm a big girl."

She gave me another hug. "You're doing well. Remember to write about all of this."

"I will."

"And we'll just hope there are no ax murderers following you online who read about you being alone tonight in the house," she said.

My eyes widened, and Ella giggled. "Don't be paranoid. Write about the alone part tomorrow. Good night, Soph."

I stood at the door until she got safely into her father's car. I was happy to see she made it without any ax murderers intercepting her—unless it wasn't her father but a murderer at the wheel. Or maybe the murderer was in the backseat, or waiting for them in their garage at home, or—

I closed the door and locked it as they drove away. I now had to fight the urge to push furniture against the door. That wouldn't help much, and in fact it might block my way if the ax murderer was already in the house.

I didn't want to be alone, but it was still good to see the two of them together. When her parents had first separated, when Ella was fourteen, she'd sworn she'd never talk to him again. It was brutal for everybody, but especially for Ella. She was an only child, so I'd always been like her sister. Apparently, her much older, overly responsible sister. But how would she ever have gotten through that without me? I didn't even want to think about the number of phone calls in the middle of the night, and the sleepovers, and the tears we'd shared.

That was the worst time of Ella's life—and one of the worst times of my life as well. But she'd gotten through it.

We'd gotten through it together. And I'd get through tonight too, but maybe I'd call her in the middle of the night. She really did owe me a couple dozen of those calls. And she might get a few of them tonight.

DAY 20

I'd written my review of the movie on my various social channels. I was shocked at the number of people who actually considered it a "classic" movie. *Gone With The Wind*, *Casablanca*, *The Sound of Music* and *The Wizard of Oz* were classic movies. This one was really pretty bad, I thought, and that's what I wrote. One guy was so unhappy with my review that he unfollowed and unfriended me, but not before he posted an Instagram picture of him holding a DVD of the movie.

More disturbing than that person's reaction or even the movie itself was a posting from Luke. He had given the *movie* two thumbs down and *me* two thumbs up for watching it. I thought long and hard about what I should say as a response, even typing in a couple before deleting them. I decided the best response was no response.

It bothered me that he was following me, but in some ways it would have bothered me more if he wasn't. It didn't help that he seemed to be having fun without me. I'd been creeping him on Facebook. He and his friends were just hanging around, going to the beach, staying out late, and the pictures looked happy. He looked happy. Was that what people looked like when I wasn't around to be responsible?

Now that the sun had risen it was time for me to blog about being alone the previous night. I was pretty sure Luke would read it.

It wasn't the best sleep I've ever had, but I managed to fall asleep finally. Before I could go to bed I went from room to room, carrying one of my father's golf clubs. I checked each door and window to make sure it was locked. I even checked the sliding doors a second time because sometimes they're not locked even when you think they are because the lock button jams. I slid in the wooden bar as an extra safety precaution.

What surprised me was how much noise my house made in the night. Things creaked and groaned and settled in a very unsettling way that sounded like footsteps. Then there were some voices outside around two in the morning—probably some stupid teenagers like the McNabb twins from two doors down coming home. And I don't care if the McNabb twins read this—you two are idiots. That's basically not an opinion but a fact. Jessie and John McNabb are idiots. Please feel free to post, retweet, favorite or like that comment.

The worst wasn't what was outside but what was inside. When I pulled that mask out from under the couch and threw it on the table, it stayed there. Ella didn't take it home, and I forgot about it. Well, forgot about it until I walked into the room and caught sight of it out of the corner of my eye—it was glowing in the dark. My heart leapt into my throat and then almost stopped beating completely. How was I supposed to know that the white parts of the mask glowed in the dark?

Once I realized that, I put the mask in the freezer. And then put a chair on top of the freezer to weigh it down or at least sound an alarm if somehow the mask pushed its way free.

Okay, maybe that's stupid—correction; it was definitely stupid—but that is what horror movies are all about. They aren't about smart or logical or reasonable or thinking. They're about irrational feelings and fears. All those things come back to haunt you—no pun intended—in the middle of the night in an empty house.

I hit *Publish* and then decided I'd take a picture of the mask and post it on Twitter and Instagram. First I'd have to take it out of the freezer.

DAY 23

"Okay, so what's today's different going to be?" I asked as Ella and I drove along.

"Isn't it a bit obvious from the way I asked you to dress?"

I was, as requested, wearing running clothes and sneakers.

"I'm smart enough to figure it's some sort of running thing. And judging from the way you're dressed—heels, a skirt and fully made up—I'm also assuming you're not going to be joining me in this one," I said.

"Think of me as cheering you on from the sidelines. Soph, you know how I feel about running. I only do it if something is chasing me or I'm chasing something. Remember what I said, that if a bear was chasing me, I'd run very fast, but if I was chasing Shawn Mendes, I'd run even faster."

"The singer?"

"Do you know another Shawn Mendes?"

"Doesn't he always seem to have a girlfriend, or two?"

"They are nothing to worry about. They are nothing more than place holders."

"You want to explain that to me?"

"Those girls are simply holding on to the role of his girlfriend for the time being. Wouldn't it have been a little bit creepy if he wanted to marry somebody who hadn't turned eighteen yet?"

"So he's just waiting until you turn eighteen?" I asked. "Don't you think there might be one or two other things that are in the way?"

"Careful what you say or I just might find somebody else to be my maid of honor," Ella said.

"I'm honored," I said.

"You could even wear those shoes."

"My running shoes?"

"White for weddings and they're *so* white. Are they brand new?" Ella asked.

"Not that new. I just take care of them."

"So they're washable, right?"

"Of course they are. How do you think I keep them looking so good? Why are you asking about that?"

"I want to make sure they can still be white for the wedding."

"Can you at least tell me how far I'm running?" I asked. "It isn't like I can run a marathon without training."

"You don't know that unless you try it, but don't worry. It's only five kilometers long."

I felt relieved but confused. "You know I've run 10K races before."

"Of course I know, so we know you can do this. You have nothing to fear, and no time to fear it. We're here."

Ella pulled the car into a dirt parking lot. On the fence was a banner—*The Dirty Duck 5K Race.* I shook my head. It all made sense—the distance, the comments about my white shoes. This wasn't just a race, it was a *mud* race.

"Strap on your GoPro and you're all set to run."

"I don't own a GoPro."

"You still don't, but you have one to use for the day," she said as she pulled it from her purse. "Since I'm not going to be there myself, I want to be able to see every jump, obstacle, mud puddle, pit and fall you go through."

"You could always do the race as well," I suggested.

"In my heels? Without chasing Shawn Mendes? We've gone over this already. You need to pay more attention to our conversations. You're already registered, so all we have to do is get your racing bib."

There were hundreds of people ready to run. About 75 percent of them were guys, and 90 percent of those guys were jacked up and crazy and ready to go. People kept yelling and shrieking, fist-pumping and body-bumping. They were like a living, breathing advertisement for Red Bull—or possibly *against* the use of Red Bull. Some were in camo running shorts and tops. Some wore eye black to shade their eyes or had mud smeared all over their faces. Still others had mud smeared all over *everything* visible. A few had been taking turns doing full-body slides through a big mud puddle just off to the side of the starting area. Weren't they going to get enough mud soon enough?

"Runners, take your marks!" the announcer called out through the bullhorn.

Everybody shuffled forward, pressing close to the starting line. I reached up and clicked on my GoPro. Now I was ready to go.

⁂

I'd posted an edited version of the GoPro footage on YouTube. I'd stopped three times during the race to tweet and post pictures to Instagram. That wasn't just about keeping my promise to document my differents on social media, but because I needed to rest. Something about running through deep mud, climbing over obstacles, swinging on ropes and running up hills for almost five kilometers can take it out of you. The uphill part was confusing since it ended at the same place it started but somehow it had seemed like the whole race had been uphill.

There was only one thing left for me to do now. I went to the laundry room, where I'd left my clothes to presoak in the sink after I peeled them off. It was hard to believe how much mud was embedded in them. Beside the sink sat an overflowing hamper of dirty clothes that belonged to my brother and father. They both would need clean clothes when they got back. I thought I would just throw in a load, but I stopped myself. This was a test—not of them, but of me.

I slopped my clothes out of the sink and into the washing machine and dumped in a double load of detergent. Between that and the presoak, there was a chance the mud and stains might come out.

I'd already wiped down my shoes and even used an old toothbrush to get the mud out of the treads. They were badly stained, and I wasn't sure if the machine wash would get them clean. I went to drop them in, then stopped. They certainly weren't what they'd been before the race. They might never be that again. And that was all right. I'd *earned* those stains. I closed the lid, started the machine and walked away, still carrying my mud-stained shoes. I guess I'd have to buy another pair of white shoes when Ella and Shawn Mendes got married.

DAY 25

"You look revolting, repulsive and repugnant," Ella said to me.

"Look who's talking! Have you looked in a mirror?"

"I could also add vile, vulgar and horrific to describe you."

"I guess I should take all of those as compliments," I said.

"You really should," she said. "You look, well, zombie-like—there's no denying it."

I pulled the car into the parking lot. Turning off the engine, I adjusted the rearview mirror so I could get one more glance at myself. An amusing and hideous image looked back at me.

Both Ella and I were dressed in rags and made up to look like zombies. The clothing had been easy. We'd taken scissors to some old pieces and added stains, including rubbing in ashes from the fireplace. The makeup had taken much longer and was done by an expert.

She was a professional who did makeup for movie stars and celebrities but also special effects for TV shows and movies.

One of her claims to fame was that she'd personally done many of the "decomposed corpses" on CSI. She had worked on our faces, necks and hands for over two hours, laying on rubberized makeup and applying special latex "wound" features to make our flesh look like it was rotting. It was quite impressive in an incredibly disgusting way.

Ella had found this woman through social. She was the friend of somebody who was following us, and when Ella put out word that we needed somebody to make us zombie-like, she'd volunteered.

"The only problem I can see with you is that you don't really *smell* like the walking dead. What are you wearing?" Ella asked.

"Chanel No. 5."

"You love those old-school scents, don't you?"

"I do."

It was one of my favorites—one of my mother's favorites. When I smelled it, I thought of her. I used my supply sparingly, usually only for super special things, because there wasn't much left in the bottle. Today, dressed as I was I felt so self-conscious that I wanted something special so I'd put on a dab. There wasn't much left in any of the bottles of perfume she'd left behind. I knew that when they were gone I could just go out and get more, but these ones were special because they were hers.

"You might be the best-smelling zombie alive," she said.

"Thanks, but technically, aren't we supposed to be dead?"

"Okay, you're the best-smelling zombie dead." Ella looked at her watch. "We better get going. We don't want to be late."

We climbed out, I clicked the remote to lock the car, and it beeped. I liked the beep. It meant it really was locked and I didn't have to go back and check—although sometimes I still did it a second time just to be sure.

A couple of people looked in our direction as we passed and then did double takes. Although our ripped clothing was partially covered, our faces were visible. I waved and offered a smile to a little girl with her mother, both of whom were looking at us. The girl hid her face against her mother's side.

"Sorry," I said as we passed. "It's just makeup."

We kept walking. Ella turned to me. "Good thing you told them that, or they would have thought we were *real* zombies."

"I can't believe that some people really do believe in zombies," I said.

"You mean you don't?"

"I have enough trouble believing in you half the time," I said.

"I'll take that as a compliment."

Carefully, so as not to disturb the makeup, I pulled up my hoodie and Ella did the same. There was no point in drawing attention to ourselves. This was all supposed to be a surprise until the moment it happened.

As we moved toward our destination, we saw more and more people. We tried to keep our faces down and looked away from those who came closest.

"I just wish I'd had this getup the night you were home alone after the horror movie," Ella said.

"Oh, that would have been lovely."

"I could have come up to the sliding-glass door and just pressed my face against it, and you would have looked and—"

"But I know you wouldn't have done that," I said.

"Yeah, you're right. I wouldn't have done that to you. Still, it's interesting to think about it. It's a shame your brother is still away with your father, or we could have gone and scared him after this is over."

"Okay, that *would* be fun."

We tried to move faster, as our time frame was getting tighter. "I should have parked closer."

Ella looked at her watch. "We're going to be okay. It's just up ahead, and I don't think it's started yet. At least, I don't hear anything."

We arrived at the edge of Dundas Square. Nothing had started. We were on time. We'd made it.

There were people crisscrossing the open plaza or standing in couples and groups, staring up at the big outdoor screen showing music videos. Others sat on the edge of a stage.

"Do you see anybody?" Ella asked.

"I see lots of people, but no zombies," I said. "Are you sure it's supposed to happen here and now?"

"I'm sure—well, pretty sure. After all, if you can't trust a zombie, who can you trust?"

"I'm not sure if the words *trust* and *zombie* have ever been used together in the same—"

Music suddenly came on. Loud. I recognized the very first notes of the song—"Thriller." I looked up at the screen. There, thirty feet tall, was Michael Jackson, red-and-black leather jacket, red pants and zombie makeup.

A cheer went up, and zombies started to materialize out of the crowd.

"Come on!" Ella yelled.

We ran toward the stage, threw off our hoodies and tossed them aside to reveal our costumes. The stage was already filling up with zombie dancers as we ran up the steps. We moved into the third row and started to dance, as behind us on the screen the characters did the same dance moves. Back and forth, across the stage, trying to dance with everybody else, doing the moves we'd practised last night, the moves we'd fooled around with since doing a skit in eighth grade.

Below the stage, on the square, there were so many people, some dressed as zombies, others not, some dancing along while others just stood there and cheered. This was amazing, and I was part of it—a zombie "Thriller" flash-mob dance!

DAY 26

I couldn't believe how many people had responded to the flash-mob pictures and videos. We hadn't filmed or taken any of the pictures. We'd found some images online and retweeted, re-Instagrammed and reposted them on Facebook.

One YouTube clip somebody had put up had been seen over five thousand times. I was responsible for eight of those views. It was hilarious seeing Ella and me up onstage, even though anybody who didn't know it was us would have recognized us.

It had taken me longer than usual to publish my blog because typing this time was really hard. I looked down at my nails. They were long fake acrylic nails. They were painted bright white and overlaid with a design—tuxedos. Each finger had a black bow tie and two black buttons below it.

This was a simple, strange and completely unexpected different. Not just unexpected for me—all of them had been—but unexpected for Ella too.

After the flash mob we'd gone back to have our zombie makeup removed. Our makeup expert, Anastacia, was also into nails, and she'd convinced us to let her do ours. These were incredibly impractical. I had trouble not just typing, but also making food, doing dishes and even punching in phone numbers. The agreement was that I'd have to keep them on for the rest of the day.

I looked down at the nails again and wiggled my fingers. Ten teeny-tiny tuxedos danced on my fingers and thumbs, and I couldn't help but smile. Maybe I'd keep them on for a second day. Just because.

DAY 29

Ella came into the house, carrying her overnight bag.

"So am I assuming you're actually going to be staying here tonight as planned?" I asked.

"I think it would be best if we both stayed here tonight. No leaving, no walking and definitely no *driving*."

Did the emphasis on the word *driving* mean something?

"You're welcome to stay as often and as long as you want, as long as you don't have a horror movie or a scary mask in that bag."

"I have many things." She unzipped her bag and pulled out a bottle. I was surprised.

"Do you like vodka?" Ella asked.

"You know I don't drink."

"And is that your plan for the rest of your life?" she asked.

"Of course not."

"Then once you get to college, you might have a glass of wine or a beer sometimes?"

"I've *had* wine before."

"When did this happen, and why don't I know about it?"

"Well, it was at dinner at my aunt's house last year at Christmas." I paused. "I really didn't like it. It tasted bad."

"Well, this is vodka, and apparently it doesn't taste like anything," Ella said.

"Apparently?"

"It's not like *I've* ever tried it. You know I'm not much of a drinker myself. I liberated it from my father's liquor cabinet. Somebody gave it to him as a present a few years ago. My father doesn't drink vodka or much of anything else."

"Your father is smart and responsible."

"And tonight we're going to be smart and responsible drinkers. We're going to stay in your house, get into our jammies, watch some Netflix and have a few or maybe a few more than a few drinks. Well, what do you think?"

I hesitated.

"There's nothing wrong with being a little bit out of control as long as the situation is in control," she said.

"I don't want to drink."

"It isn't about drinking. It's about allowing yourself not to be in control all of the time. Isn't it tiring to always have to be in control?" she asked

"Sometimes."

"Well, your choices are, you can watch me drink and you can be the sober, responsible, boring big sister, or you can join me. What's it going to be?"

"Fine, I'll do it. Maybe I'll have just one or two."

DAY 30

I opened one eye and then shielded it with my hand, blocking out the light. Why was it so bright...wait...it was morning. And it all started to come back to me. My eyes adapted to the light and focused a bit more. I was lying on the living-room carpet. Ella was just a few feet away on the couch, sound asleep, snoring a little—she usually snored when she slept. I always found her snoring a little cute, although the drool running down her cheek this morning took away from the general cuteness. Maybe I should take a picture of her snoring and drooling and put it up as *my* new cover picture, I thought.

I tried swallowing, but my mouth was really, really dry and tasted terrible. It felt like I had a dirty sweat sock in my mouth. I looked down and was relieved to see both socks still on my feet. Ella's feet were tucked under a blanket, and for all I knew she could have been wearing only one sock.

I pushed myself up to a sitting position, and then I saw it sitting on the coffee table, staring at me. The bottle of vodka—or at least the remains of the bottle. I got up, and on unsteady legs walked over and picked up the bottle. I gave it a little shake so that the liquid swirled around inside. There was still almost half a bottle. That meant that we had either drunk or spilled the rest. Judging from the taste in my mouth and the fogginess in my head, I didn't think we'd spilled much.

I stared at the bottle. How could something so clear, so transparent, so *water*-looking, be *so* bad? I had the feeling the eagle on the bottle was staring back at me and, worse, was taunting me. Just how much had I drunk to be thinking such strange thoughts? There was only one thing to do in response.

I carried the bottle to the kitchen sink, tipped it over and watched the clear liquid run out of the bottle and down the drain. Then, just to make sure it couldn't get back up, I ran cold water to flush the sink and force it down into the sewer, then pushed the plunger in place to seal it in. If I'd learned anything from that horror movie, it was that the monster was never as dead as you thought it was.

I bent over, turned my head and started drinking from the flow of water. I kept drinking and drinking, hoping to rehydrate myself or at least wash the sweat-sock feeling out of my mouth.

Satisfied, I opened the kitchen cupboard and tossed the empty vodka bottle into the recycling bin. At least the bottle could do some good now.

My phone started ringing, and it felt like I was being stabbed in my left eye. I rushed over and grabbed it before it could stab me a third time.

"Hello!" I practically yelled and then regretted the volume of my voice.

"Soph, are you all right?"

It was my father.

"Sure, I'm good. I'm just a little...a little—"

"A little hungover?"

I was shocked. I didn't want to lie to him. "Yeah, I guess a little. How did you know?"

"I'm one of your friends on Facebook and followers on Twitter, remember?"

Then it came to me in a rush of jumbled memories. Ella and I had gone online before we'd gone to sleep so that I could post what was happening, although I had only the vaguest memory of what I'd written.

"Sorry for drinking."

"You're eighteen. In some places that's the legal drinking age so it's not the worst thing."

"Sorry you had to find out that way," I said.

"Most parents never find out—or find out when their child staggers home drunk or is arrested or ends up in the hospital or something worse. This was much better."

"Really? Did I say much?"

"A couple of pictures—"

Okay, I remembered taking some pictures.

"—a few tweets and a blog with a few typos."

"I'll fix those," I said. If I didn't just take them down.

"Take care of yourself first. Drink plenty of water," he said.

"Already on it."

"Is your head hurting?"

"A combination of being hit with a hammer and stabbed with a knife."

"A couple of aspirins will help."

"Sounds like you have some experience with this," I said.

"I wasn't always old. I did a stupid thing or two myself when I was your age."

I heard my brother's voice in the background.

"It sounds like your brother is up. How about if you find the aspirin, and I'll fix him breakfast and call you back later today."

"Sounds good. Love ya."

"Love you too, honey, and remember, be safe but not too safe."

I hung up the phone and went to my iPad. I was more than a little worried about what I'd written.

My first tweet had gone out at 3:13 AM. It was obvious that we were well into the bottle at that time.

With my old BFF, Ella, and my new BFF, Mr. Smirnoff!

Attached was a picture of me, Ella and the bottle. Ella and I both had goofy looks, and the eagle on the bottle really did look like it was smirking.

Okay, it could have been worse. It had been retweeted seventeen times and liked twenty-three times. That was more than almost anything I'd tweeted before. That was good, and it wasn't really that bad a tweet or picture of me. I looked a little glassy-eyed, but all right—good, in fact. Better than Ella did. I hated myself for even thinking that or caring.

Next was the blog.

It was short and rambling, with more than a few grammatical errors and a spelling mistake. Obviously, drinking and writing were far less lethal than drinking and driving, but not any better. I could always fix it. No, I'd leave it and add what I was thinking now.

Last night I did a new different. I drank vodka. I've never drunk vodka before. Really, I haven't drunk much of anything before. Last night my friend and I drank too much. This morning I'm going to be drinking even more. Water, lots and lots of water, to go with the aspirin to ease my headache. I'm going to keep doing differents. Some are better than others. This one wasn't worth repeating.

DAY 33

"So have you ever been in the back of a police car?"

"Of course not!" I exclaimed.

There were no handles on the door, so I couldn't get out even if I wanted to. I was trapped, separated from the front seats by a metal mesh screen. I was wearing a bulletproof vest, and over that an orange sash that said *CIVILIAN* in big white letters, as if that was the only thing that revealed I wasn't really a police officer.

"I didn't think so. You don't look like a hardened criminal," the younger of the two officers—"just call me Todd"—said. He didn't look much older than I was. He reminded me of a kid at the eighth-grade dance who'd borrowed his father's sports jacket, except that tonight he'd borrowed his father's uniform and gun.

"You know that some of our ride-alongs are part of the Scared Straight program," the older officer—"call me Sarge"—said.

"I don't know what that means."

"Teenagers at risk of getting in trouble with the law or who have already committed minor offences experience what it's like to be in the system," Sarge explained. "They get picked up at home, thrown in the back of the car, processed, printed and tossed in the cells for the evening."

"The hope is that they can be scared straight and won't become criminals," Todd explained.

"I've never even had a detention at school before," I said.

"Never?" Todd asked in disbelief.

"Never. From kindergarten until I graduated."

"I had *days* in high school where I was given more than one detention," Todd said.

"That I believe, Junior," Sarge said. "The first time they put you in my car, I thought *you* were here for a ride-along."

"I guess when you get to be as old as you are, everybody looks young," Todd said.

"I wish I could still give you a detention every now and again. So, Sophie, why are you doing this? Are you thinking about a career in law enforcement?"

"No, never!" I exclaimed and then thought better of my reaction. "Not that there's anything wrong with being a police officer. It's just that I'm not good with unpredictable things."

"We get a lot of unpredictable," Todd said. "Unpredictable and dangerous is what gives us our rush."

Sarge laughed. "Ninety-nine percent of what we do is predictable, and as exciting as watching paint dry."

"And the other 1 percent?" I asked.

"That's where we earn our pay and gray hair."

The non-gray hair on my arms stood up.

"But probably tonight the most exciting thing that's going to happen is watching Todd eat. That's dangerous, unpredictable and a little—*did you see that*?" Sarge asked, his voice suddenly changing.

"Saw it. On it."

"Saw what? On what?" I asked.

They ignored me as Todd barked out letters and numbers into the radio and the sergeant put on the red lights.

"He's not stopping," Todd said.

"He might not have noticed or doesn't think we're after him. Give him the siren as well."

Todd hit the siren. It got my attention and that of the driver of the car. His brake lights flashed, and he pulled over to the curb and came to a stop. We pulled in a couple of car lengths behind him. The officers left the lights on but turned off the siren.

"What did he do?" I asked.

"Erratic driving. He veered badly out of his lane," Todd explained.

A staticky voice came over the radio.

"No wants, no warrants, no warnings on that plate," Todd said.

"Don't let your guard down because of that. Remember, SOP—standard operating procedure." Sarge turned to face me through the mesh. "I'm going to open the back door as I get out. That doesn't mean you should get out of the car. I just want you to be *able* to get out if you need to."

"Why would I need to?"

"You won't, so don't get out, okay?"

I nodded. He didn't have to worry.

They got out, and Sarge opened the back driver's-side door, leaving it slightly open so it wouldn't relock. I fought the urge to pull it closed to seal me inside, safe and sound.

Sarge walked directly to the driver's door of the vehicle. Todd walked to the other side, stopping well short of the vehicle. I'd seen enough TV police shows to know that's how they did it—Todd covering the sergeant in case the driver pulled a gun or something. How silly was I to even think about that? The driver of the car was probably some soccer mom who'd wandered out of her lane because she'd dropped her cell phone or the baby in the backseat had cried or—

Sarge had reached through the open window of the car and was struggling, wrestling, with the person at the wheel! Todd charged over, reached in and grabbed the man as well, and the two of them pulled the man out the window and tossed him onto the ground. The man bounced to his feet. He was big, much too big to have been pulled through the window of a car. He tried to run, but Todd grabbed him by the neck. He spun around and punched Todd!

Todd staggered backward, and at the same instant the sergeant tackled the man, knocking him to the ground. Todd recovered and leaped on top of him too. Lightning fast, Sarge whipped out his cuffs and locked them onto the man's wrists. He and Todd hauled the man to his feet. They dragged him to the police car and threw him on the hood with a thud. The car shook, and I reacted by screaming! The man, his head pressed against the car, looked up, saw me and, despite his situation, winked at me.

❖ ❖ ❖

I turned out the light, but I didn't think I'd be able to sleep. There was still adrenaline in my veins. How many nights had I sat at home watching TV shows that involved the police? Today it was like I'd been in one. Maybe it was that leftover adrenaline talking, but it wasn't completely crazy to think it would be pretty exciting to be a police officer.

I reached over and turned on the light. Maybe I'd just add a little more to my blog before I went to sleep.

DAY 35

I continued to get notifications throughout the day. Of everything I'd posted, nothing had gotten such a reaction. I was amazed at how many times the picture had been retweeted, favorited, liked and commented on. My Facebook friends now numbered over 1,600, Twitter was over 600, and Instagram had leaped to 743 followers. Apparently, being dressed in a Wonder Woman costume was a big hit. I went back into my blog entry.

It was like being part of the biggest, strangest, Halloween party ever, and that party was taking place in the middle of the summer. But of course it wasn't a party, it was a convention—a Comic convention. While costumes weren't mandatory, they certainly were plentiful. Every single cartoon and comic superhero from Star Wars, Star Trek, Lord of the Rings, Game of Thrones, Hunger Games, X-Men *and* Teenage Mutant Ninja Turtles *seemed to be represented there. I really did like the Turtles and always had a soft spot for Leonardo—I used to watch the show with Oliver and pretend I was April O'Neil, ace reporter. She was fun and full of adventure and wasn't afraid of anything. I admired that about her. I still do.*

Ella insisted we couldn't truly go to Comic Con without costumes, and she picked out ours. If I'd known what she was going to pick, I might have fought harder. I went as Wonder Woman, and she was Catwoman. I couldn't believe how little material went into my costume and how tight hers was. But once we got there, I learned that those are the two essential elements of any female costume—tight and revealing. Well, those are the ones that get attention, and we got attention. In some ways, though, we did seem a little old school compared to those dressed as Katniss and Storm.

The males—who far, far outnumbered the females—had their share of costumes featuring less-than-usual amounts of clothing, and somehow it seemed like those who most should have covered up didn't. Superman, as far as I can remember, had a six-pack and not a keg.

Of course, that was only true of some of the Supermen. There were lots and lots of them. Plus dozens of stormtroopers—who would want to be a stormtrooper?—and enough hobbits to actually find the one ring to rule them all.

Before we went I was pretty sure I knew what sort of person goes to a Comic convention. And I guess I was right and wrong. There were some people who were a little fanatical—after all, painting yourself completely blue like an avatar or green from head to toe like the Incredible Hulk is not a sign of what most people would call balance. And why were there so many Incredible Hulks to begin with? Is there something in the male psyche that makes them want to wander around shirtless, in ripped pants, while painted green and making grunting sounds? Maybe a bunch of these guys were computer nerds who live in their parents' basements and have never had a girlfriend because they are too busy playing online video games.

What surprised me more than those people were the participants who were so different. As we started talking to people, we found husbands and wives, people with kids and grandkids. We talked to people who were lawyers, mechanics and doctors—including my family doctor. Weird.

He was dressed as Gandalf the Grey. If he hadn't come up to me, I never would have recognized him underneath the robe and fake beard. Obviously he didn't feel bad or embarrassed or he wouldn't have come up to say hello. In fact, he was very proud of his costume and talked about some of the other conventions he'd been at across the continent. I don't think I can ever see Dr. Watson again without thinking about him in costume—and I'm almost due for my annual physical. Maybe it isn't so bad to have a physical done by a wizard. Thank goodness he wasn't dressed like a Smurf.

He wasn't the only person we ran into that we knew. One of our high-school teachers—I guess now that we've graduated, a former high-school teacher—Mrs. Van Norman—was dressed as Catwoman as well. She was, however, Catwoman dressed in so little material that it seemed like Ella was dressed in a full-length robe by comparison. She was so friendly and gave us both a big hug. I had trouble making eye contact as we talked, but then realized there was no place else safe to look at her.

What I also noticed were the looks she was getting. Every single guy who passed by stared at her. Apparently, little-dressed Catwoman was equally appealing to hobbits, stormtroopers, Captain Americas and those not dressed as anything except themselves.

It's easy to make fun of something you've never done. What I saw on the surface was a bunch of people dressed in strange costumes.

What I found underneath the costumes were people who were friendly and kind, committed and knowledgeable, passionate and playful. Maybe a bunch of them are nerds. Maybe I'm one of them.

I'm not going to go to next year's convention, but I'm not saying I won't ever go again.

Let the force be with you. Live long and prosper. Cowabunga, dude. May the odds be ever in your favor. And always remember, not all those who wander are lost.

DAY 37

"Okay, let's go over the signals one more time!" the spotter yelled from the back of the boat. Ella was sitting beside him while I lay on my stomach on top of the tube, bobbing up and down.

We went through the signals for *faster*, *slower*, *stop* and *go home*. He was satisfied I knew them.

"And this one is the signal for *I want to throw up*," Ella said, putting a finger in her mouth.

"That doesn't happen—well, hardly ever," the spotter said. "Are you ready to go?"

I nodded, gave a thumbs-up and tried for a smile. The signal worked, and the engine noise increased as the boat started to move slowly away. The slack in the rope lessened as it snaked through the water, getting taut, and then I was jerked forward. Instinctively I tightened my grip on the handles.

The boat went faster. My feet skimmed the surface as the tube skipped along. We continued to travel in a straight line away from the shore and out into the middle of the lake.

I noticed well off to the side a smaller boat and a couple of guys fishing. They waved, and I let go of one of the handles and gave a weak little wave back. I was relieved that one hand was enough to hold me in place.

We continued to pick up speed. The spray in my face increased, the tube started bouncing a bit more, and I held on tighter. Still, it wasn't that bad. I could handle this—and then the boat suddenly cut sharply to the side. I kept on going straight and skipped over the wake of the boat and into the air! As the boat continued to turn, I picked up speed, until it seemed like I was going to get in front of the boat!

The driver changed course again, and as the rope went slack I slowed down dramatically. I'd weathered whatever had happened. I was fine. The rope started to snake through the water, getting tighter and tauter, and I knew what was coming next. This wasn't going to be good. I gripped the handles as tightly as I could, and the tube and I jerked forward. Desperate to hang on, I felt like my arms were almost being yanked from their sockets!

Back and forth the boat cut, and I shot over the wake and into the air, bouncing and landing and almost tipping over with each landing. My arms were aching, my fear fueling the adrenaline that kept me from flying off. I wanted him to slow down, I wanted him to stop, but I couldn't signal without releasing a hand, and if I did that, I couldn't possibly have stayed on.

The boat pulled an even tighter turn, going in a circle, and I continued to gain speed as I was slingshot around the boat in a big circle, moving faster and faster. How long could I possibly hang on?—I flew off and skipped across the surface, twirling and barrel-rolling, spray everywhere, until I slumped down into the water. I gasped, swallowed some water and then bobbed back to the surface again. I was okay, I was okay. I had to let them know.

I looked all around, trying to figure out which way was which, searching for the boat—there it was! I raised my arms above my head to signal them.

The boat completed its turn and came back toward me. I treaded water and waited. It was coming up, as planned, on my right-hand side. It would be here to pick me up in a few seconds. There was only one more thing I needed to do. I reached down with both hands and pulled up my bathing-suit bottom, which had been dragged down to below my knees.

The boat came up slowly. Ella was at the very front, waving and whooping, a big smile on her face. Despite it all I smiled back. And why shouldn't I? I'd survived, and the different was done! The boat came up beside me, and the driver turned off the engine.

"Nice work!" the spotter called out.

"Most don't last nearly that long," the driver added.

"You did good, Soph!" Ella yelled.

I swam the few strokes over to the boat, and the spotter reached down and pulled me up, and I climbed into the boat.

"Thanks for your help," I said. "Do you have enough gas to do another run?"

"Of course we do," the spotter said.

"You want to go again?" Ella exclaimed.

"Again, yes. Me, no. It's your turn. Different isn't just for me. Well?"

"Challenge accepted."

DAY 38

I looked at that one message—again. It had all started on my timeline the previous evening. Some guy named James had said something about my Wonder Woman photo and then the picture of me in my bathing suit from the day before. He'd asked me out. I didn't know him, and I wasn't going to be dating anybody anyway, so I messaged him back. **Thanks but no thanks.** What followed was a message telling me I was nothing more than *a tease* and what did I expect when I was posting things where I was *parading around in a bathing suit*?

First off, it was a bathing suit covered by a life jacket, and second, what was I supposed to wear to go tubing, a raincoat? And third, even if it was a bathing suit, I had the right to wear what I wanted without being judged, harassed or bothered by some idiot.

I'd messaged him back and said just that. Big mistake. His reply was angry and filled with mean things. I was shocked that anybody would say such things. Nobody had ever talked to me that way in my entire life.

I just hadn't expected anything like this. People had made lots of comments—on my timeline, in private messages, in tweets—but almost all were supportive and kind and funny and playful.

I looked back at the message. There was only one thing to do. I deleted it and then blocked James. With friends like him I didn't need enemies.

DAY 39

The clock on the wall continued ticking away. It was nineteen minutes to midnight. It had been such a long day. Maybe time hadn't stopped, but it certainly had slowed down over the last twenty-three hours and forty-one minutes.

I looked down at my phone. It was turned off, as it had been for twenty-three hours and forty-two minutes, since one minute before midnight the previous day. Turned off and dead, it was still important. It was such a part of my life that it felt more like a *part* of my hand than simply something I *held* in my hand. It had been paralyzed, still, unmoving and unresponsive for the entire day.

Of course, it wasn't just my phone that had been off. The house phones had all been unplugged. All three televisions had been unplugged to stop me from inadvertently clicking one on. My iPod and tablet had been put away. I'd just turned my computer back on a few minutes earlier to get it ready to go, but I had deliberately walked away before I could be tempted.

Today's different was certainly different. It had sounded so simple, not much more complicated than leaving my bed unmade—although even that had turned out to be harder than I ever would have imagined. With this different, there were no heights, no speed, no possible way to get hurt or even scared. I didn't even have to leave the house. Actually I *couldn't* leave the house. It was that simple. For twenty-four hours I couldn't communicate with anybody. No direct conversation, no telephone calls, no texts, no Facebook. Nothing.

After being loaded up with so much social media, this was even harder. Like I'd been given a free sample of drugs, gotten addicted and now had to go off them cold turkey. Ella was right—social could become so addictive, so quickly.

I'd put a notice on all my social media sites letting people know I wouldn't be online in any way for the next twenty-four hours as my different for the day. With people so used to instant responses, it could be worrisome for them if there weren't any.

I'd also had a conversation with my father just before midnight. He was following me on a couple of platforms, so he probably would have known anyway, but I wanted to make sure so he wouldn't worry when he couldn't get in touch with me. As well I wanted to talk to him before the cone of silence fell over top of me. I guess I *needed* to talk to him.

I normally checked in with my father regularly. With him gone, it had been four or five texts or calls every day. It wasn't him checking on me as much as me checking on him and Oliver. I needed to know they were all right. I always did.

For a while after my mother died I needed to know where my father was at all times. Oliver and I were only one parent away from being orphans. When he was even a few minutes late coming home from work, it made me panic. I'd stand at the front window waiting, staring, praying that the next car that turned onto our street would be his. I'd make bargains—*please let his car be in the next five*. I couldn't help going through all the terrible things that could have happened to him, and then I'd start thinking about what would happen to us, how I'd care for my brother, how we would survive.

But at least we had somebody who would adopt us. My aunt Janice and uncle Art would take us in—thank goodness for them. Even thinking about it now made me start to feel nervous again. It was a creeping sense of uneasiness rising up from my stomach and into my chest. I took a deep breath and shuddered it away. I wished it had been that easy back then.

This was definitely the longest I'd gone without talking to my father in years and years and years—no, forever. I knew he and my brother were fine. I knew that. Still, my father was going to be my first call.

Ella had added one more element to the challenge, and that was the reason the TVs were unplugged and the iPod put away—I wasn't allowed to even *hear* human voices. Not in movies, on TV or even in music. It had gotten to the point over the last few hours that I'd started talking to myself just to hear a voice. The annoying McNabb twins from down the way had been yelling at each other, and it had been like music to my ears. Even the sound of an ambulance going by a few streets over was reassuring—there were still other humans on the planet.

The first eight hours hadn't been hard. I'd been asleep. Waking up to complete quiet in the house, my first reflex had been to reach for my phone to check for messages and notifications. I'd fumbled on my night table looking for it before I remembered. Luckily, I'd put it across the room, turned off, with a little note on top to remind me.

Fixing breakfast and eating in silence wasn't a chore as much as a pleasure. At least at first. Then it got eerie. It got to the point where I would have even enjoyed having my brother here annoying me. I read the paper—I *was* allowed to read. We got the paper delivered to the door—something I'd accused my father of being old-fashioned for doing. Thank goodness for old-fashioned.

I'd read somewhere that forcing people to do nothing was a form of torture, that it contravened the Geneva Convention—the agreement on the rights of prisoners. So instead of doing nothing, I'd done the things I was allowed to do—exercised, read, exercised some more and written by hand on paper.

I'd spent an hour on the treadmill and elliptical machine. Normally, I would have listened to music or at least watched TV while I was exercising. The quiet made it harder. With nothing to distract me, I could only think of two things as I ran—why am I running, and when can I stop?...why am I running and when can I stop?...why am I running and when can I stop? It had become a mantra, a chant inside my head that had finally started to come out of my mouth. I had liked hearing my voice.

My favorite activity throughout the day was eating. I'd eaten breakfast, followed by a second breakfast that would have made a hobbit proud. I'd had brunch, lunch, dinner and then a really, really big snack. By my own estimate, I had ingested enough calories to make an NFL lineman feel bloated and full.

Throughout the day I'd gone back to reading the paper, and eventually I'd read it from cover to cover, including the business section and even the obituaries. I'd started on the obits simply to fill time. Then it had gotten to be more than that.

First I saw her picture. She had dark hair. She was pretty, middle-aged, with warm eyes looking out at me. Her name was Brenda Carson. She was thirty-five, a mother of three. That made her two years younger than my mother had been when she died. I read through the obituary. She was a mother, wife, daughter, sister, aunt, friend and teacher. My mother was a teacher and all those other things too. Brenda was survived by her parents and one sister. My mother was survived by her parents and one sister.

I'd never seen my mother's obituary. I'd just assumed there had been one. I thought about asking my father. I'd hardly ever asked him anything about her. I wasn't really sure if I was protecting him or me.

Being alone and not allowed to communicate had meant I had time to think. I'd thought about who my mother was and what I knew about her. I'd realized there were gaps, and even things I thought I knew but maybe really didn't.

I couldn't seem to get her out of my mind. I'd tried. The exercise, the food and even reading a book. None of it had worked. The book I'd been reading made me cry like a baby.

I'd known enough about the book to expect somebody was going to die—somebody *always* seemed to die in these stories—but it had still opened the floodgates. I wasn't sure if that was because I was already feeling vulnerable or simply because the book was so well written. Maybe both. Was I crying for the character who wasn't real or the real mother who had died? Was I crying for the people left behind in the book or the people left behind in my house?

I looked up at the clock again—it was one minute to midnight! I'd lost track of the last few minutes and almost overextended the different.

I pushed the button at the top of my phone and held it until the phone started coming back to life. It wouldn't take very long to be ready to receive and make calls. I had to admit I was curious to see what had happened on my different platforms over the past twenty-four hours. In the past few weeks I hadn't gone more than thirty minutes when I was awake without checking or posting, tweeting or blogging, replying or calling, or—my phone started to ring!

Instinctively I went to answer it, then stopped and looked at the clock at the top of the screen. It was still 11:59. I wasn't going to be caught one minute or even a few seconds early. It rang and rang and rang. I could see it was Ella calling, but I couldn't answer until it was the next day—*12:00 AM* flashed on the phone.

"Ella!" I screamed into the phone.

"Soph, you're alive!"

"I'm alive. Did you miss me?"

"Me and everybody else, it seems. You won't believe how many posts and hits you have. You have to go online right away and let everybody know you're all right."

"I'm going to call my father first."

"Won't he be asleep already?" Ella asked.

"He might be, but I think he'd want to hear from me. I'll put something online before I go to bed."

"Good. Now get a good night's sleep. After all, you're going to need it for tomorrow's different. Good night."

I hung up, waited a few seconds and then called my father. Talking to him would make sleep so much easier.

I punched in his number and it started to ring and—"Hey, Soph," my father said, his voice barely a whisper.

"Hey, Dad, I didn't wake you, did I?"

"Of course not. I was waiting for your call. Your brother tried to wait up as well, but he just fell asleep."

"I just wanted to say good night."

"Good night, Soph. And thanks for calling."

I put down the phone. I exhaled deeply. That eleven-year-old inside of me could relax. Now I'd be able to sleep—right after I wrote a little bit about the day before.

DAY 40

"Turn right here!" Ella yelled.

I cranked the wheel and made the turn into the alley. There were fences on one side, and on the other were the backs of stores, some parked cars, and dumpsters and garbage cans and piles of trash. It was much darker in the alley than it had been on the street. We edged forward.

"Why are we here?" I asked.

"We all have to be somewhere."

"Somewhere, yes. In a downtown alley at two in the morning, not necessarily."

"That's where and when he wanted to meet."

"Where *who* wanted to meet?" I asked.

"Slow down—I think the parking spot is just up ahead."

I slowed down and also hit the door-lock button.

"There it is!" Ella said. "Park under that big moon painted on the back of that building."

I drove into the empty spot.

"Turn off the engine, and let's get out," Ella said.

"I'm not doing anything until you tell me why we're here. We're not going to break into a building, are we?"

"Of course not. We're just dressed like cat burglars." Ella pulled something from her purse. "Put this on."

It was a black woolen hat. I pulled it on and was now completely dressed in black from head to toe, as was Ella.

Ella got out of the car. I hesitated for a second before I turned off the engine and got out as well.

"So if we're not committing a crime, why are we dressed in black in an alley in the middle of the night?" I asked.

"I *did* say we weren't breaking into a building. I *didn't* say we weren't going to be committing a crime. Well, technically a crime."

"What exactly does that mean?"

"Some people consider it a crime, and others consider it art," Ella said.

I was going to ask her to explain when I realized the answer. The entire alley—the fences, walls of the buildings and even the dumpsters—were covered in bright colors, streaks and patterns and pictures, some crude, some beautiful and detailed.

"We're going to be doing graffiti?" I asked.

"I think the correct term is street art. We're going to be street artists."

"But neither of us is able to draw stick people."

"And that's why we're not doing it alone. I think that's our host," she said as she pointed down the alley.

There in the shadows was another shadow coming toward us. He was carrying a large bag over one shoulder and a small ladder on the other. He also was dressed in black, and his face was shielded and shaded by a hood pulled over his head.

"Hey!" Ella called out.

"Are you Ella and Sophie?"

"We are. So you must be Night Crawler."

His name was Night Crawler? We were here in the middle of the night to meet a guy named Night Crawler?

"That's my street name." He stepped out of the shadows, and I stepped back and gasped. He was wearing a skeleton mask. He pulled the mask off. He was young—not much older than us—and he was smiling.

"Pleased to meet you both," he said, and we shook hands.

"Should we have masks as well?" Ella asked.

"This is more for dramatic effect, more for my persona than anything else," he said.

"I guess that's sort of like a superhero," I said.

"Or a supervillain," Ella added.

"So should we call you Night Crawler?" I asked.

"Cody will do. I'm not hiding my identity from you two. Some of the people who own the walls of the buildings aren't so thrilled. So are you ready to go?"

"Ready and willing," Ella said.

I wasn't necessarily feeling either of those things.

He started walking, and we fell in beside him.

"You really worked hard to find me," he said.

"I'm fairly persistent," Ella said. "And social media is a powerful tool."

"I got messages from a bunch of people telling me you were looking for me."

"I figured I'd just put out the word and you'd hear about it."

"How did you even know to look for me?" he asked.

"I asked some people who would be the best street artist to go out with, and your name kept coming up."

"I guess I should be honored."

"Us too. Thanks for the invitation to join you."

"It's nice to have company. Usually it's just me, the rats, cats and a few raccoons. The only people I see are the ones stumbling home after a night of drinking and partying. And, of course, there's the occasional police car."

"Is that a problem, the police?" I asked.

"There's always a danger. They've arrested some of my friends. That's why we do it in the middle of the night, dressed this way, and why I've chosen to hide my face."

"How long have you been doing this?" Ella asked him.

"About two years. I started when I was in my first year of art school."

"You went to art school?" I asked.

"You sound surprised. Don't you think this is art?"

"Of course it's art. I was just surprised because I thought street art would be more...I don't know, organic, than done by an artist trained at some school or college."

"Believe me, this isn't anything they're teaching me in school. I have one more year before I graduate with my degree in fine arts and design," he explained.

"That's impressive," I said. "Do you want some help with the stuff you're carrying?"

"Sure, you can take this." He took the big canvas bag off his shoulder and handed it to me.

I was surprised by how heavy it was. "What's in here?"

"There are cans of spray paint, brushes, ropes and assorted stencils."

"Stencils?" I asked. "What are they for?"

"You'll see soon enough."

"The stencils I understand," Ella said. "What's the deal with the rope?"

"Are either of you afraid of heights?"

Ella laughed. She knew very well how I felt about heights. I looked at the ladder on his shoulder. No matter how he extended the ladder, it wasn't going any higher than my height.

"No problem with heights at all," I said. Ella nodded approvingly.

⁘ ⁘ ⁘

I pressed myself flat against the roof of the building as I carefully looked over the edge. Night Crawler had a rope tied to his waist and to a chimney as he perched on the ledge below us. We were a lot higher than a stepladder. Cody had used the rope to move us from one building to the next along the attached roofs, getting us higher in steps until we were now on the top of a five-story building. The scene below was silent and still. There were no moving cars and no people, although it was still brightly lit by the streetlights. In fact, it was so bright that I was sure Cody would be visible to anybody who did go by.

He was using a big stencil—sort of a large cardboard cut-out—to do his art. He taped it to the wall and then spray-painted, the cardboard protecting places that weren't supposed to be painted and the cut-out part creating the image on the wall. This cut-out was of a big dancing raccoon—which was one of Night Crawler's favorites to use. It was a great symbol, a creature wandering around the city at night, making his mark and avoiding people.

Before we'd started to climb, we'd done a few pieces below. It didn't look like much when we were doing it. But once the stencil was pulled away, the image was revealed. Ella and I got to do one of the raccoons almost completely by ourselves.

Cody also did a couple of sayings—Art in a Frame is Like an Eagle in a Cage, with a big eagle painted on the side, and a second that he said he had written just for me. It was simple—Do More, Feel More, Be More. I had to admit it was pretty amazing. I was thinking of making it my header on Twitter, so I took a picture of it.

Cody was working on the sixth image, so it looked like a chorus line of dancing raccoons. If it looked good from up here—upside down—I could just imagine how fantastic it would look from below, when you could take in the whole perspective. After he was finished I wanted to take a few pictures to share on social.

"You're handling the height pretty well," Ella said.

"I've been higher. Besides, this *is* pretty cool."

"Cool enough to take Cody up on his offer to come out another time?" she asked.

"I think I might."

Ella gave me a big smile, and we exchanged a high five.

Cody had asked us to do street art a second time. He'd also asked me out for a coffee, and I'd politely turned him down. He'd seemed okay with it. More okay than Ella had seemed. It wasn't that she'd said anything, but she'd given me a quick look that I caught out of the corner of my eye. Did *she* want to go out with him? Was this her feeling invisible? It wasn't like I'd said or done anything. Then again, maybe I was just imagining things.

There was a car coming up the street. There hadn't been that many, though more than the occasional vehicle. It was the middle of the night, but it was also the middle of the city, so some traffic was inevitable. Cody had told us not to worry, because generally people looked straight out of their windows, seldom up.

The car was moving very slowly. Maybe he was a delivery guy. I could have used a pizza right about then. Adrenaline and fear created appetite, and I felt like I was starving.

A bright light came from the passenger side, and the beam of light swept along the storefronts, as if someone was searching for the right address. Suddenly the light shot upward and started to sweep across the tops of the buildings.

"It's the police!" Ella gasped.

Cody desperately started to scramble up the rope, trying to get off the ledge and onto the safety of the roof. Before he could reach the top, the beam of light swept over him and then past—they hadn't seen him! But then the light retraced its route to catch him, brightly, squarely, in its angry eye.

A metallic voice boomed out, "Stay where you are!"

Instead, Cody pulled himself over the edge and flopped down, practically landing on top of the two of us.

"We have to get moving!"

Ella jumped to her feet, and I scrambled to do the same. The beam of light shone above the edge and just caught the tops of our heads. I ducked down.

Cody grabbed his bag and started running, but instead of heading back the way we'd come, he ran along the tops of the buildings in the opposite direction. We ran after him. There were more than a dozen stores in a row, each roof not more than a few feet higher or lower than the one beside it. We jumped down or climbed up as we went from building to building, the gravel and pebbles on the roofs sounding under our feet as we moved.

Suddenly Cody skidded to a stop, and we did the same. We were at the end of the row of stores, a laneway separating us from the next row of stores.

"What now?" Ella asked. "Do we go back?"

"Not back," Cody said.

He tossed his canvas bag across the gap, and it landed with a thud on the roof on the other side of the lane.

"It's not that far," Cody said.

He backed up a dozen steps.

"He's not really going to—"

Before I could finish my sentence, he'd run to the edge and launched himself, practically hanging there in midair before crashing down on the other roof and rolling. He jumped back onto his feet.

"It's not far," he hissed. "I made it easily. You can do it."

I looked at Ella, who was looking at me. I shook my head.

"I agree," she said. "I'd rather be arrested than break my neck."

"What do *we* do now?" I hissed over at Cody.

"Lay low—wait them out. They'll get called for something important."

I thought about my ride-along and how the sergeant had said that sometimes something important didn't happen all night.

"Besides," Cody said, "they're probably not going to climb up after you."

"Probably?"

"No guarantees."

"What about your ladder?" I asked, thinking maybe I could entice him to come back over. "Don't you need it to get down?"

"I've got another length of rope in my bag. You can use the ladder. Besides, it isn't mine. I grabbed it from one of the backyards a couple of blocks over. Good luck," he said.

He turned and started away.

"But Cody, you can't just leave us here!"

He stopped and turned around. "Actually, Cody isn't my real name." He turned back around and ran off. He jumped down to a lower building and disappeared, although we could still hear his footfalls as he vanished into the dark.

"Nice, very nice," Ella muttered.

"What do you expect from a guy named Night Crawler?"

"So what now?" Ella asked.

"I guess we wait and hope they don't climb up to get us."

DAY 41

I startled awake, and it took me a few seconds to remember where we were—on a roof downtown, in the middle of the night. Wait—it wasn't that dark anymore. I pulled out my phone—it was five thirty. I was glad my father and brother were still away. It would have been hard to explain—*Sorry, sleeping on a roof—be home in the morning.*

Ella had her head on my leg. Her eyes were closed, and she was asleep and gently snoring. She looked so peaceful that I almost didn't want to wake her, but we had to get moving.

"Ella, wake up," I said, shaking her gently.

"I don't want to get up, Mommy," she mumbled.

"*Mommy?*"

Ella's eyes popped open, and she instantly seemed to figure out that not only wasn't I her mother, but we were also far from her bedroom.

"Do you think they're gone?" she asked as she got to her feet.

"We can only hope." I crept over to the corner edge of the building, where I could look down. The streets were coming alive with vehicles, but there was no sign of any police car.

Slowly, quietly, we made our way back across the tops of the buildings. The energy and fear and adrenaline of the previous night were replaced by creaking, cold joints and sore backs from sleeping on the cold, gravel-covered roof. We reached the store where we had gotten up onto the roof. I lowered myself over the edge and dropped to the lower level. Despite how gently I tried to land, there was still too loud a thud. Ella dropped down beside me, and the sound echoed across the rooftop.

We continued to move, trying for quiet but not quite succeeding. We went to the edge, and I peeked over.

"The ladder is still there."

"Do you see anything else?" Ella asked.

"Nothing. We're all alone. Let's go."

I stepped onto the ladder and started down. Ella was immediately behind me. I reached the ground and—

"Good morning."

I spun around, jumped and screamed. It was Sarge and Todd.

❖ ❖ ❖

For the second time I sat in the back of a police car. The fact that the doors didn't open from the inside meant something much more significant this time. Ella was trying her best to remain brave. It wasn't working so well. Todd and Sarge were in the front seat, the police radio adding a soundtrack like every scene of every police TV show and movie I'd ever watched. I just wished this was one of those scenes instead of real life.

"You weren't who I thought would come down that ladder," the sergeant said.

"Not quite who I expected the Night Crawler to be," Todd added.

"Neither one of us is the Night Crawler!" I protested. "Honestly!"

"We know that, but we saw the raccoons and knew it had to be him up there with you," Sarge said.

"He was, but he ran and left us."

"Is this guy a friend of yours?"

"A friend wouldn't have left us," I said. "We don't even know his real name."

"So we're supposed to believe you wandered up that ladder, dressed in black, and accidently bumped into him?" Sarge asked.

"No, I arranged to meet him," Ella said.

"Maybe you can arrange for us to meet him."

"I contacted him on social media. He agreed to take us out for the night."

Todd laughed. "So you sort of went with this Night Crawler on a ride-along, like you did with us."

"Pretty well," I said.

"So this was one of the differents you're doing," Todd said.

"Exactly."

"Except this one was illegal," Sarge added. "Are many of your activities illegal?"

"No, of course not!" I said. "Right, Ella?"

"Technically, I'm not sure if we did anything illegal tonight. It's not like you *saw* us painting any graffiti."

"Well, if you want technical," Sarge said, "I do see paint on your hands."

I looked at my hands and then Ella's.

"That's just, um, circumstantial evidence," Ella said.

"Great, I have a teenage lawyer in the back of my car," Sarge said. "So, lawyer, how about if we forget about the vandalism charge?"

"That would be great!" she exclaimed.

"And instead we'll charge you with trespassing, intent to commit burglary and, in your case, attempting to avoid arrest by taking flight."

"What?"

"You ran last night. That could easily be seen as attempted escape or even resisting arrest, don't you think?" he said to Todd.

"Definitely. We could even find some other things to charge them with. We could have their car ticketed and towed while we're taking them down to the station to book them."

"Is that technical enough for you?" Sarge asked Ella.

"More technical than I'd like. Sorry, sir."

"Good. Now there's one other way we can play this," he said. "You can both promise that you'll never do this again and that no more of your little different things will involve breaking any laws, and we'll let you off with a warning, and you can both be home in time for breakfast."

"You'd do that?"

"Sophie, you seem like a good kid." He turned to Ella. "You too. Good, but mouthy."

"I am a bit too mouthy sometimes. I know that and—"

Sarge put a finger to his lips to silence her. He got out of the car and opened the back door for us. I climbed out and Ella hurried after me, bumping into me.

"Thank you so much," I said.

"Yes, thank you," Ella echoed.

"You know this whole different thing is interesting," Sarge said. "But remember, Shakespeare said *to thine own self be true.*"

"You're quoting Shakespeare?" Todd said.

"Yeah, you got a problem with that?"

Todd held up his hands like he was surrendering.

"Do you think because I'm a cop I can't be cultured?"

"I'd never say that," Todd said.

"How about you two?" he asked, turning to us.

"No, sir, definitely not, sir," Ella said, and I nodded enthusiastically in agreement.

"It's a quote from *Hamlet* where Polonius is talking to his son Laertes, and believe me, I'm old enough to be the father of all of you."

"You're actually a lot *older* than my father," Todd said.

"It's not too late for me to put *you* in the back of the car. What that quote means is that a person needs to remember who they are. Sophie, you're not a criminal. You're a good person. Don't lose that while you gain other things."

"I'll try to remember. Thanks for that as well."

They got back into the squad car. "Now go home, and no more trouble," Sarge said through the open window.

They drove off, leaving us standing beside my car. Todd reached out of the window and gave a little wave goodbye.

"Well, on the bright side, you got in a new different," Ella said.

"And almost got arrested doing it."

"No, you don't understand. Doing the street art was one different. Nearly getting arrested was a second. That's two differents in one day. Congratulations!"

"And you didn't even count the sleeping-on-the-roof part," I added.

"Then that's different times three. Great work!"

DAY 43

I posted the picture to both Twitter and Instagram. It was me, but it wasn't me. Well, at least the hair wasn't me. It was my eyes and my face looking out from beneath bright-purple hair. I'd had to choose between purple, orange and green, and I had to keep my hair this color for a week. The purple brought out the blue of my eyes, making them an even darker, deeper blue.

At first Ella had tried to convince me to actually dye my hair. Instead we went with a compromise involving purple hairspray and purple hair chalk. Ella did the honors. We went into the garage, and she covered me with an old sheet so only my head and hair could get bombed. Ella wore an old pair of work coveralls and a plastic shower cap on her hair, and we both put masks over our mouths and noses and ski goggles to cover our eyes.

Using a comb to part my hair, she sprayed it strand by strand. It was slow and smelly and hot and messy as the purple aerosol drifted through the air and landed on the concrete floor. I was so glad I'd moved my car out before we started. Finally she used the purple hair chalk to get individual pieces that were missed.

Washing up took almost as much time as the hair job. We just tossed the sheet and the overalls. They could have been washed, but they weren't worth much, and I was afraid they'd contaminate the washing machine. Ella had purple hands—mine had been covered by the sheet—and we both had purple on our necks and any places on our faces that weren't covered by the masks and goggles. It really took a lot of scrubbing to get our skin clean, and I started to worry that this was a lot more than temporary. Those fears were put to rest when Ella fluffed and patted me down and a purple rain came tumbling out. Then I thought I was going to be leaving a trail of purple dust wherever I went, but after the initial downpour it settled into almost nothing.

We'd gone out to the mall afterward. It may be true that blonds have more fun, but there is no question that purples get more attention. We got lots of looks. Some people looked amused. A number of guys made comments and started to talk to us. It was like my purple hair let them know we were friendly or freaky or simply available for conversation. Older people—especially older women—didn't look very happy. If looks could kill, I would have been at least badly wounded.

Strangest of all was what happened at a store where we shopped all the time. We were followed by two women lurking an aisle away, pretending to shop while looking at us out of the corners of their eyes or peeking around corners or through the shelves. It was rather unnerving. In the end Ella had gone over and asked them why they were following us, and they confirmed who they were—store detectives. Apparently, purple is the color of thieves. I decided then I wasn't going to be shopping for the rest of the week.

My phone buzzed, and I looked. My picture had been retweeted twice and liked three times on Twitter and liked twelve times on Instagram. Social media moved at the speed of light. I couldn't help but wonder if orange would have gotten more or less reaction.

DAY 44

I looked up from my food just as my brother suddenly looked down at his plate. I was having a chicken Caesar salad, and they were having another can of stew. My father had decided that variety involved different types of stew. They'd returned the night before, and it was good to have them home. But obviously he hadn't picked up any cooking tips at my aunt's place.

Once again I caught my brother looking at me and then glancing away as I looked at him.

"You seem pretty fascinated by me," I said.

"Not really."

"Then why do you keep looking at me?"

He shrugged. "Since when do you think you're so special that everybody is looking at you?"

I almost answered that close to two thousand people on Facebook and over fifteen hundred on Twitter and Instagram were looking at me, or following or friending me, but realized that would have sounded pretty egotistical.

"Not everybody is looking at me, but you definitely are."

"Maybe he's just glad to see you because he missed you," my father suggested.

"Yeah, like that could happen."

"Well, I was just thinking that you don't look any different," Oliver said.

"You might have noticed that I have purple hair."

"Your hair is different. That doesn't make *you* different," he said. "Besides, it's already starting to fade."

It had faded over the past 36 hours. I was grateful and a little sad. Purple wasn't bad.

"You know that just because you're doing different things, it doesn't mean you're actually different," Oliver said.

"I'm not sure if I agree or disagree." I wondered if there was something else he wasn't saying. "Dad's right—you really did miss me."

"Did that purple dye seep into your brain as well as onto your hair?" he asked.

"Well, if that's not it, then what is it? What's bothering you?"

"Nothing is bothering me...well, almost nothing."

"Then what is it?"

"It's just that you don't *need* to be different."

"What do you mean?"

He looked very uncomfortable.

"Come on, what do you mean, Oliver?"

"Look, don't let this go to your purple head, but you're not the worst sister in the world."

"So you don't mind me ordering you around and acting like your *mother*?"

"You could stop ordering me around, but that's really just the same as your hair. It's just something you *do*, not something you *are*."

"That sounds deep."

"Look, all I'm saying is that Luke was an idiot for breaking up with you."

"No arguments from me there, although I'm surprised you'd say that."

"I think lots of things that I don't necessarily say. I'm eleven, not stupid, but you're stupid if you think you have to be different to get him back."

"I'm not trying to get him back."

"Good, because you're *way* too good for him."

"Wow, that's the nicest thing you've ever said to me."

He looked like he was blushing!

"You said a nice thing to me. I'm going to come over and give you a big hug and a kiss and—"

He jumped up from his seat and ran off screaming.

"You're not getting away that easily!" I yelled and ran after him. "You're definitely going to get hugged and kissed!"

DAY 45

Oliver was recklessly hopping from one swinging step to another, connected to the cables linking one tree to the next. He got to the treetop platform at the other end, climbed up and hooked one of his carabiners onto the cable around the tree and released himself from the cable running between the trees. He let out a gleeful scream of joy that echoed through the trees, then looked over and waved. I waved back. I felt happy for him. And relieved he was back on sort of solid ground, if the treetop platform could be considered either solid or ground. He was so much faster and agile than us, and I thought he was frustrated at our lack of speed and skills.

"He makes it look easy," Ella said.

"Ridiculously easy. By the way, thanks for not objecting to my brother coming."

"I like your little brother."

"Really, would you like to have him? I could give him to you."

"Well, not right now, but later. After all, he is my backup plan if Shawn Mendes doesn't come through."

"Somehow he seems as unlikely a husband as Shawn Mendes does."

"Why? Is your brother married?" She looked over at him. "Are you married?" she yelled over.

"What?"

"He doesn't listen, just like any husband I've ever met," Ella said to me.

"Oliver, honey, are you married?" she yelled again.

"Are you on drugs?" Oliver called back.

She turned to me. "Isn't that so sweet that he's interested in my well-being? He's cute, and I'm sure he will listen to me because I'm older."

"That hasn't worked for me."

"You're just his sister. I'll be his wife."

"Okay, then let's talk about a dowry. Make me an offer," I suggested.

"Come on, you wouldn't give him up for the world, would you?" Ella asked.

"He has his moments, but not really."

I guess that's why I'd wanted to have him with us. I'd missed him, and it wasn't long before I'd be going away to school.

"He's really quite the little monkey the way he scampered along the ropes and aerial apparatus," Ella said.

"He's pretty fearless," I said.

"You're afraid enough for both of you. It's like you inherited a double dose of scared, and he lost out on his portion of the fear factor."

I'd thought about that—how because I worried and was so responsible, he didn't need to be, and my father didn't need to be either. Did my father do so little because I did so much? Had I stopped him from becoming more of a parent because I had filled that role? Was I an enabler of him doing less? Or was he genuinely not capable of doing more? So far he hadn't done much more than open a can of stew or run the vacuum cleaner across the floor.

"Although you aren't doing nearly as badly as I thought you would," Ella said.

"You thought I was going to do badly?"

"I arrange things that push you, and this is a push, right?"

"I'm doing pretty well, all things considered," I said.

"Not bad. Really, I didn't think either of us would get this far along the course."

"We're only two obstacles away from finishing, so I think we've both done amazingly well," I said.

"Do you want to go next, or should I?" Ella asked.

"I think me. The sooner I start, the sooner I end."

We were all wearing mandatory helmets and harnesses equipped with two cables and carabiners—special metal clips. We always had one or both of those clipped onto cables, so there was no danger of us falling more than a few feet before the cable would catch, and we could be pulled back up. So far none of us had dangled. I *hated* the idea of dangling, although far less than the idea of falling.

I clipped one of my carabiners on the cable suspended above the steps between the two tree platforms. I then unclipped myself from the cable surrounding the tree.

I stepped out on the first little swinging step, holding on to the cables as well as being clipped onto them.

We were told by the instructors who trained us that the secret was not to look down. That was impossible. If you didn't look down, you wouldn't know where your next footstep needed to be. I slowly went from one step to the next, each perch swinging as I moved, threatening to buck me off and leave me dangling.

"Can't you move a little faster?" Oliver yelled.

I ignored him.

"You know you're going away to college in a few weeks. You might want to pick up the pace!" he said.

I tried to block him out. I needed to focus on what I was doing.

"I was wrong about you not changing," he said. "You could change the way you move so slow! *That* you could do different."

I clipped myself to the next stage of the cable, checked that I'd done it right and then reached back to disconnect the second cable. Only four more swinging steps, and I'd be there on the last platform with Oliver.

"It's a really, really, really big drop if you were ever to fall," Oliver said. "Where you are must be the highest point on the whole course."

I looked over. He was lying on the platform, his head over the edge, looking down. I felt my knees get weak.

I took one more step, then on to the next. It swung back and forth before stabilizing. Then I moved on to the next, and the next, and then to the last step. With the final step, Oliver, who had stood up, offered me his hand, and I jumped up and onto the platform. I clipped one carabiner onto the platform before undoing the one on the cable. I was safely on the platform now.

"Thanks for the encouragement," I said.

"What's a little brother for? Besides, I want to get on with the last zip line. It's a lot longer than the others."

"How much longer?"

"Come and look."

We circled around the big tree. There was a large pond between it and the next tree, and I could see that the zip line extended all the way across the water to a tree way, way over on the other side. We'd already done three short zip lines. They were the worst of everything in the whole aerial course. There was that instant when you stepped off the platform and dropped down, temporarily falling until the cable snapped and you started zipping down the line. It was an act of faith to conquer your fear and step off the platform and into space.

"That *is* really long," I said.

"The longer the line, the longer the ride. Can I go now?"

"We're not going until Ella is here."

We didn't have to wait long before she was standing at our side. Without any further delay Oliver clipped himself onto the zip line. He jumped off the platform and dipped down, almost disappearing from view, and my heart jumped into my throat. He then raced along the cable, going faster and faster. I held my breath as he crossed the pond and then reached the platform on the far side. He turned and gave me a big wave.

"So you're next," Ella said.

"I could be next, or we could both just climb down the ladder on the side of the tree and walk around the pond," I suggested.

"You could do that. The old Sophie would have walked."

"The old Sophie wouldn't have been up here to begin with. My different is already done for today, wouldn't you agree?"

Ella shrugged. "I guess so."

"I'm glad you agree. I have nothing to prove. So that's why I'm going to do it."

I stepped off the platform, dropping down as my stomach lurched up, and then raced along the cable. Faster and faster, the pond now underneath, I raised my arms and started flapping them, a gigantic bird. I had no fear left. I just enjoyed the ride.

DAY 47

I opened my eyes. It was snowing. Inside the house. I blinked hard and rubbed my eyes, thinking it was just sleep in them, but—no, it *was* still snowing, inside the house, in the middle of the summer. Was I dreaming? Then I realized it wasn't snow. It was soap bubbles fluttering through the air!

I jumped off the couch and ran toward where they seemed to be coming from. More and more of them drifted down the hall. I turned the corner to find the kitchen filled with suds! They were not only floating up to the ceiling but also covering the entire floor with an avalanche as deep as the kitchen counter. I slid to a stop, almost falling as my feet slipped on the soapy floor.

"Oliver!" I screamed at the top of my lungs. Part of me wondered if he was buried beneath the suds. The biggest part knew that somehow this was his doing. "Get down here to the kitchen right *now*!"

It was all so surreal. The kitchen was covered in a deep layer of suds. It was almost beautiful, like seeing a new snowfall, peaceful and undisturbed by footprints. But it certainly wasn't quiet. A motor was rumbling—it was the dishwasher. I couldn't see it, but I could hear it. It was buried, but I knew it sat under the mountain of bubbling suds. It had to be the source of the bubbles.

I rushed in, and my feet slipped out from under me. I tumbled into the suds and slammed heavily to the floor, knocking the air out of my lungs. I pushed off to try to get up, but my hands kept slipping and slipping, and I felt a little bit panicky, buried beneath the suds. Could you drown in soap suds? I fumbled around, finally located the counter and pulled myself to my feet.

"Sophie, what did you do?"

I turned around and brushed the suds away from my face and eyes. Oliver was standing at the kitchen doorway, looking as shocked as I'd been.

"What did *I* do? You think I did this?"

"It wasn't me!" he exclaimed. "I was upstairs, playing an online game."

Still holding the counter, I edged my way to the dishwasher. I groped around until I located the latch amid the suds and turned the machine off. Within a few seconds the bubbles had stopped shooting into the air.

"You loaded the dishwasher and turned it on, right?" I asked.

"Yeah, but it wasn't like I broke it. I did everything right, so the dishwasher must be broken or something. It's not my fault."

He looked so worried that I felt sorry for him, even if it was his fault. How could it *not* be his fault?

"I squirted in an extra squeeze of soap, but that couldn't have done all this," he said.

"What do you mean, *squeezed in an extra squirt*? The dishwasher uses packets of dishwasher detergent," I said.

"I know that, but we were out, so I used the liquid dish detergent," he explained.

I picked up the plastic bottle from the counter. It was half filled with blue-green liquid. It had been completely full a few days earlier. I knew that because I'd filled it.

"An *extra* squirt?" I said.

"Well, first I filled up the two little compartments—you know, where the packet goes and where the rinsing stuff would go."

"We don't use a rinsing agent," I said.

"I know, but I figured more would only help. And because the dishes were really crusty, I figured I had to do it if I wanted them to get clean."

"If you ran it more than every third or fourth day, they wouldn't get crusty."

"I don't want to waste energy."

"It's a high-efficiency machine, so it doesn't use that much energy."

"I meant *my* energy," he said. "So because of that, I put some extra squeezes right onto the dishes to soften up the dried-on food. I wanted them to be sparkly clean."

I shook my head slowly, but no words seemed to come.

"So what are we going to do?" Oliver asked.

"First, we need to get a—" I stopped myself.

"First we need to get a what?" Oliver asked.

"You need to clean it up."

"But what do I need?"

"You'll figure it out," I said. "In the meantime, I'm going to take a nap."

"You're doing what?"

"I'm going to take a nap. You did this, so you need to fix it."

"Come on, Soph, you have to help me."

"No, I don't."

"But I don't know what to do."

"Aren't you the one who's sick of me telling you what to do?"

"Yeah, but once more would be okay."

"What would you do if this happened when I was away at college?"

"I'd call Dad."

"Then call Dad."

Keeping a hand on the counter to avoid falling again, I edged around the room through the suds, feeling like a snowplow.

"Excuse me," I said as I slipped past Oliver and out of the kitchen. I walked away on sloppy, soapy, slippery stockinged feet, not looking back.

✣ ✣ ✣

Oliver appeared in the doorway of my bedroom. He was wearing a bathing suit.

"It's done," he said.

"All of it? Even the dishwasher?"

"I emptied it and then rinsed out everything, even the little compartments, and got rid of the rest of the liquid soap."

"How did you get rid of the suds?"

"They sort of popped, and then I used a bucket and mop. Do you want to check?"

"Not me. I'm not your mother."

"But I wanted you to see how amazing the kitchen looks," he said.

"I imagine being free of three feet of suds would make it look pretty good."

"It's more than that. The floor and cupboards are sparkling. It was like I washed the floor as well as did the dishes!" he said. "Plus there's one other bonus."

"What's that?" I asked.

"I'm so squeaky clean I don't need to take a bath tonight. The whole thing worked out to be like a win-win-win situation."

"Maybe you should do that every day."

He shook his head. "Once was enough. And Soph, I'm sorry."

"Mistakes happen."

"Yeah, but I shouldn't have expected you to fix it."

"It's not just you," I said. "I expected me to fix it. I guess in some ways this was a new different for both of us."

DAY 49

The techno-pop music blared as the models cut through the bright lights and strobes, parading along the runway. We were a dozen rows back. It was pretty amazing in a bizarre way. Never had I see so many women who were so thin, so strangely dressed and so incredibly tall. I was almost five ten, but compared to them—most in super-high heels—I would have been dwarfed.

They strutted the runway, shoulders back, stick thin, and they all had the same pained expression. I suspected that look might have something to do with being really, really hungry, mixed with the pain caused by being forced into those shoes. Why did fashion models all have to be painfully thin?

"So this is new, huh?" Ella yelled over the music.

"Different than anything I've ever seen before."

This had been an easy different. It was nice to be the watcher instead of the person being watched. I'd seen fashion shows on TV, but being here in person was completely different.

"Come on," Ella said as she got to her feet.

We did a sideways shuffle along the row. It wasn't just the people on the runway who looked fashionable or strange. This was one well-appointed and oddly dressed audience. They were all done up, and while some people were just elegantly or expensively dressed, more were dressed in bizarre ways. Theirs were colorful, unique, strange fashions that would have caused people to turn and gawk if they were on the streets. Here they hardly got a backward glance.

Along with the strange clothing some of them wore makeup that would have scared a clown or shamed a goth and had hairstyles that made my previous purple seem pedestrian at best. Buzzed off, spiked up, extensions that went below the waist or piled higher than Marge Simpson would ever dream of. It had been as much fun watching the people in the lobby before the show as it was watching the show itself.

Part of me felt a little self-conscious about the way I was dressed. Of course Ella hadn't told me what we were doing, so I'd worn a pair of Old Navy jeans today. She was dressed a lot better, and if she'd told me, I could have put on a dress, at least, and some more makeup. I guess she was just doing the usual not-telling-me-to-not-worry-me thing. Or she was deliberately trying to be better dressed than me.

Strangely, my unfashionable clothes and nearly complete lack of makeup were almost a fashion statement in themselves, and Ella pointed out that we'd gotten more attention than some of the more bizarrely dressed. Here, I guess, being dressed so normally made *us* bizarrely dressed.

Ella stopped in front of a door with a sign saying *Backstage Access—No Admission to General Public* in big letters. A large man wearing a dark suit, darker sunglasses and an even darker expression stood at the door. His arms were crossed, and he looked as angry as the models. Ella leaned in close and started talking to him. I couldn't hear her above the music.

He smiled, nodded his head, stepped aside and opened the door, gesturing for her to enter. She motioned for me to follow.

"Thanks," I mumbled as I passed the man. He closed the door behind us, and it took a few steps for my eyes to adjust to the darkness in the narrow corridor.

"Ella, where are we going?"

"The dressing room. You really don't think you can be on the runway dressed in your jeans, do you?"

"The *runway*? I'm walking the runway?"

"If you haven't noticed, nobody walks the runway. You'll be strutting the runway."

I was stunned.

A stream of very tall, very skinny models bumped their way through the corridor, which probably connected the stage to the change room. For all the order out there, there was a sense of chaos here as they pushed past each other.

We entered a big room. There were dozens of models in various stages of undress, with other people helping them get in or out of their things. I felt like I wasn't just out of place, but that I was intruding. No, worse than that. It was like we were uninvited guests in the middle of a room filled with half-dressed strangers. I didn't know where to look or not look.

"You must be Sophie!" a woman called out as she rushed over.

"This is her," Ella said.

The woman took me by the hand, dragged me away and sat me down on a stool beside a dressing table.

"You're huge!" she exclaimed.

"I'm only five ten."

"I didn't mean tall, I meant big. What size are you?"

"I'm a six," I answered.

"Even worse than I thought. Nobody here is more than a zero."

"If you were a zero, wouldn't that mean you didn't exist, that you were invisible?" Ella asked.

The woman ignored Ella's comment as she scrambled around, grabbing clothing. I assumed she was looking for something "huge" enough to fit me. She turned back to me. "Why are you still wearing clothes?"

Without asking my permission, she started to remove my top, pulling it up and over my head. I was so shocked that I didn't even think to struggle.

"Shoes and jeans. Get them off, right now!" she commanded.

I hesitated, and she yelled at me. "*Now!*"

I responded, kicking them off and then standing there in just my bra and panties. I would have felt embarrassed if I wasn't standing in a room full of women who were in various states of dress and undress. It was like being in the change room in gym class except that instead of sweats and T-shirts and sneakers, they were in designer outfits and heels.

I heard a ripping sound and turned my head. "Thank goodness for seam rippers!" the woman said. She handed me the dress she'd just ripped apart. It was a little black outfit.

"Don't just look at it, put it on!"

I pulled it over my head and tugged it down. Despite the ripped-out seam, it still hardly fit, clinging to me like a second skin.

I looked at Ella. "How is this going to work? It's all ripped and—"

"Put this on over top," the woman said. She handed me a golden sweater. "The colors work, and the sweater will cover most of the rip. Go and get shoes," she ordered, gesturing to the side. "Black. The higher the heel, the better. It will create the *illusion* that you're thin."

Ella walked with me to the rack. It was taller than me and filled with shoes.

"Just how did you arrange this?" I asked.

"You have five followers in the fashion industry, including Donna Venture."

"Who's that?"

"Come on, you have to know who she is. She's one of the biggest designers in the country. That dress that got ripped, the one you're wearing, is one of her creations. It's probably worth twenty-five hundred dollars."

"My whole wardrobe isn't worth that much," I said.

"No surprise there," the stylist said as she appeared out of nowhere. She was holding a pair of gold heels—very high heels. "I decided gold was better. Put them on."

She turned and rushed away.

I slipped into the heels. They were the right size, even if they weren't the right height. I now towered over Ella, teetering and threatening to tumble over.

"You, over here!" a woman yelled.

I turned and pointed at myself, and she nodded.

I walked in a wobbly way toward her. She gestured to the chair in front of her. I was just grateful to sit down before I fell down.

"Who did your makeup?" she demanded.

"Nobody…me, I guess."

"You shouldn't do that anymore. At least there isn't much work to undo. Thank goodness most people have no idea how to apply makeup, or there wouldn't be work for professional makeup artists."

She started applying makeup. I assumed she was doing to me what would match the rest of the models. That would mean angry black swaths on my eyes and lips and dark patches on my cheeks. "Normally, your makeup would have been applied before the clothing went on," she said.

"Hair, we need emergency hair over here!" the stylist yelled as she returned.

Almost instantly two women were on top of me, pulling and pushing and pinning my hair. I was about to say something when I was assaulted by a rainstorm of hairspray, and I closed my eyes and mouth instead.

"That's as good as we're going to get," the dresser said. She grabbed me by the arm and pulled me up to my feet. "Get into the line."

"Where's the line?" I asked.

The stylist rushed away without answering, taking the two hair stylists and the makeup artist with her.

Ella shrugged. "Just follow the other models."

There was a line of models bumping by each other in both directions along the narrow corridor. Those moving in one direction were being attended by dressers, who were making last-minute adjustments to their outfits or hair as they moved. Those going the other way were already peeling off layers of clothing. Most of the models were female, but an occasional male was interspersed among them. Nobody seemed embarrassed by being semi-naked. Even in school change rooms, I was never that comfortable.

"So now you know how I feel," Ella said.

"What do you mean?"

"Compared to them, you're the short, chunky one."

I was going to say something about how neither of us was short and chunky, but in this strange, alternate universe we were both. Despite my height and heels, the models were almost all taller than me, and there was no question that they were much, much thinner. At best I felt like a rather plump ostrich among giraffes. Actually, that wasn't right, because I was pretty sure the model in front of me was dressed in ostrich feathers, so there was at least one other ostrich—a very, very tall ostrich with an angry expression.

"I'm going out front now," Ella said.

"Couldn't you stay with me?" I begged, suddenly feeling very alone in a room filled with people.

"I need to be out there to take pictures. Just remember, throw your shoulders back, look like you're either angry or constipated, and you'll fit right in."

"That's encouraging."

"Just think of yourself as the plus-sized model."

"That's not funny."

"It wasn't meant to be funny. Maybe this different will give you some insights into how the rest of the world sees you, or maybe how it sees *me*. Some of us never get to be the tall, thin one."

"Ella, that's not how—" Before I could finish, Ella had turned and walked away, leaving me in the line. I was almost more shocked by what Ella had said than anything that was happening around me. She had sounded so, well, angry—and it was like she was angry at me. That couldn't be, could it? It didn't matter, not right now. I had to focus on what I was doing, or I was going to fall flat on my face. Who wore heels this high anyway?

The line slowly bumped forward, and I wobbled along with it. In front of us was a heavy dark curtain. That had to be the curtain that led to the runway. Oh my goodness. I'd have rather walked along a real runway, dodging planes, than do this.

The model directly in front of me turned around. "You'll do fine."

"Thanks."

"I've been following your blog," she said.

"You have?"

"You've done some pretty cool things."

"My friend Ella arranged them. She arranged this."

"Donna told us. You're lucky to have a friend like that."

"I am." She was right, and I had to remember that. Ella was putting in an amazing amount of work, and she was doing it for me.

"Don't worry," the model said. "Just walk behind me. Ignore the crowd and the photographers. Act like they don't even exist. Focus on the runway. And the most important thing, if you're going to trip, do it on the way *off* the stage instead of on the way *on*."

I couldn't help but laugh.

"Believe me, I've done it more than once. The longer the legs and the higher the heel, the more potential to trip. If you do fall, just jump up and continue moving forward like nothing happened."

"Thanks for the advice."

"Tell you what. If you trip, I'll trip too. We'll make it look like performance art." She gave me a squeeze on the shoulder. "Don't worry. You'll do fine."

"Thanks for that even more."

The techno-pop music got louder as we got closer to the stage. Finally we came up to the curtain, and my new friend got a signal and disappeared through the curtain. I stepped forward. I was next. I felt sweat dripping down my sides—a true flop sweat—and wondered if they'd charge me for dry-cleaning the dress.

"Next," the man at the curtain said.

He pulled the curtain aside, and I froze. I was instantly assaulted by bright lights and blaring sound.

"Go," he said and gave me a little push.

I stumbled, staggered, took a deep breath and started to walk. The sounds and sights were much more intense out here. I felt like I was being assaulted, almost slapped in the face. The music blasted, the spotlights were brilliantly bright, and dozens of flashes started to go off.

I took a few steps, teetering on my heels, desperately trying not to tumble over. I didn't need to think about my expression. Desperation and scared probably came off as angry and hungry.

Up ahead was my new friend, strutting. I tried to match her pace and mimic her walking. As I went down one side of the runway I passed the models coming back the other way. They looked straight ahead. No eye contact with either me or the audience. I tried not to think about how the audience was reacting as they saw me, but it must have been clear to everyone that I didn't belong there. It was like that game, Which of these things doesn't belong?

My new friend made the turn and started on her way back. She actually looked at me, smiled and reached out a hand.

"Work it, girl!" she said as she reached out, and we exchanged a low five as we passed each other.

I got to the end of the runway. I kept my pose for a few seconds and gave them my best stink-face look. I did a slight twirl and headed back the other way.

Deliberately, throwing my shoulders back, strutting, I couldn't help myself. I started smiling, then laughing, then waving at the audience, and then, in six-inch stiletto heels, I started skipping. There was a roar from the audience and an explosion of flashes, then cheering as I stumbled, almost falling off the runway. I was positive I heard Ella scream out. I got to the end of the runway and pushed through the curtain to backstage—safety.

I'd done it! I'd made it! I'd survived! My new friend grabbed me and gave me a big, big hug.

"You did it, girl! You did it!"

A couple of the other models offered congratulations.

"We don't have time for this!" It was my stylist. "Hurry up. That was only your *first* outfit."

"My first! You're kidding! I have to go out there again?"

She smiled. "Just putting you on. Go and get dressed. Somehow we'll have to stagger through the rest of the show without you."

"Thank you. Thank you so much."

"My pleasure."

I started to walk away.

"And dear," she said. I stopped and turned back.

"You really are a beautiful young girl. How about in the future you leave Old Navy clothes to old sailors? You can do better than what you wear. You *are* better."

DAY 50

Today I rode a horse, a camel and an elephant. And I drove a race car and a fire engine. Of course, they were all made of plastic and metal and were in the mall. Today my different was so simple. All I did was ride the kiddie rides. Something I hadn't done since I was probably five years old.

Ella stood there taking pictures as I bounced up and down or the wheels spun around or the engine roared. At least the animals were big enough—although my legs almost did touch the ground on the horse. With the race car I had to stuff myself inside, and it made a roaring sound, and the fire engine had a bell. At Ella's insistence I rang it repeatedly as people walked by. Little kids pointed and laughed. Some adults smiled or pointed, and others very pointedly tried to look away and pretend there wasn't a teenage girl riding the kiddie rides in the mall. Or they simply looked at me like I was crazy or with a level of disgust. I liked the ones who smiled. I wondered if it had been me six weeks ago watching somebody do this, how would I have reacted? I don't like to admit it, but I think I would have been one of the people looking disgusted.

I was happy that it made most people smile. I liked that little kids pointed and laughed. Those who gave me disgusted looks at least were reacting. I was more bothered by those who didn't look. I decided I wasn't going to give them a choice. I started ringing the bell on the fire truck even louder. I honked the horn on the race car and smacked the elephant on the rump, trying to get it to go faster. I yelled like a cowboy when I was on top of my horse.

Ella said that sometimes I just take myself too seriously. Of course, she's right. At first it did feel embarrassing to be sitting on those rides, but there are worse things than being embarrassed.

Some of the differents I've done have been scary. Others have been exciting. Some have been thrilling. Today's was just harmless and playful, and it made some people laugh. And in the end it made me laugh. That wasn't such a bad different to do today. And besides, I think I looked pretty good riding on that elephant.

DAY 51

I sat on the edge, my feet dangling in the water. In the rubber wet suit, the water felt okay—not cold. I'd never really liked cold water and was amazed at those people who could just run to the edge of the dock and throw themselves into the lake, often without even checking to see if it was cold or if the water was deep enough or if there was something in the water like a floating log.

I always wanted to check. I *needed* to check. And even then, I'd ease in slowly, testing the water to make sure it wasn't too cold or there wasn't something dangerous just below the surface where I couldn't see it. I guess that was like me with most things.

I moved my flippers back and forth, kicking up little currents beneath the surface of the water. The water was clear, and I could easily see all the way to the bottom. It wasn't that deep—at least, not here.

"Check to make sure your tank is secured," the instructor said. He was an older man who was heavy in the middle. With his black, slick wet suit and his thick mustache, he looked like a walrus.

I'd already checked the fastening twice, but I didn't say that. I checked a third time.

"Remember, I'm going to be right there with you, so there's nothing to worry about," he said.

"I'm not worried."

He looked a little doubtful. "You know I've been doing this for twenty-five years and never lost a person."

"That's good to know."

"My youngest student was five, and my oldest was an eighty-five-year-old woman. She did it on her birthday. So don't be worried."

"I'm not," I said.

"Your friend said you'd be a bit nervous and that I had to make sure you were comfortable. There's nothing worse than panicking down there."

"Thanks, and I'm not going to panic. I appreciate you checking and also Ella telling you that, but I'm okay."

"Just do everything the way we practiced on dry land. Breathe normally through the mouthpiece. Now, put on your mask."

We both dipped our masks in the water, drained the water back out and put them on. He looked at my mask and made a slight adjustment.

"Next the regulator," he said.

I put in the mouthpiece, which had been dangling from my shoulder, and pushed the regulator button to allow oxygen to flow. In through my mouth, out through my nose, was how

I was going to breathe. I took my first breath, and it flowed very normally.

My instructor slipped into the water and then gestured for me to do the same thing, and I did. We both sank slowly to the bottom. He gave me a thumbs-up, and I returned the signal.

He started swimming, and I followed. It was just like I'd been taught, just like I'd thought it would be. My instructor did a little spin, and I did the same thing. He went down, and I went down. He went up, and I went up. It was a little game of follow the leader. It was simple and safe and really pretty cool.

I looked up and beyond him. There was activity in the water in front of us. There were lots of them, and they were moving, and we were headed straight for them—and then I remembered. It was the seniors' aquafit class taking place in the shallow end of the pool. And as we got closer I could hear the music—or at least feel the bass pounding through the water.

For my first dive I didn't have to worry about sharks or reefs or currents or wrecks or boats. All I had to do was avoid a dozen dancing seniors thrashing around to a disco beat. The next time I did this, if I did it again, I'd be in the ocean. Would scuba diving in an actual body of water constitute another different, or at least a half different?

I remembered the underwater camera dangling from my left wrist. I had promised Ella I'd take some pictures. I'd argued there wasn't much to shoot. I'd take a couple of my instructor, maybe one showing the depth marked on the side of the pool, a couple of selfies, of course, and one more thing. I turned away from my instructor and headed for the shallow end. Seniors' aquafit, here I come.

DAY 52

It was a beautiful, sunny afternoon, the perfect day for a walk in the park. Of course, being with Ella meant there was more to this than an innocent stroll. I scanned the horizon, looking for something that could be a different.

All I saw were picnicking families, kids on the playground equipment, two guys flying a kite, and a baseball game going on in the distance. I had eaten picnic meals, been on monkey bars, flown a kite and even played baseball on a team, so the different couldn't be any of those things.

Ella, as always, was keeping her plans under wraps.

"So what are we doing here today?"

"I'm looking for the leash-free zone."

"It's over there on the other side of those trees," I said.

"That's right, you had a dog."

I nodded. Our dog—Candy—had died a year after my mother. We'd all taken it pretty hard.

"We used to take Candy to this dog park sometimes," I said, "so how does this qualify as a different?"

She just smiled and kept walking. "Candy. That's a cute name for a dog," she said.

"My parents let me name her. I was only three years old."

As we got closer I could see dogs tearing around on the other side of the fence and hear them barking up a storm. The sight and sounds caused a rush of memories of being here in the park with just my mother and father, then with them and my brother in a stroller, then with just me and my father and my brother. Candy had liked the leash-free zone, and I'd liked watching her have fun. Dogs never worried about anything.

We walked through the first gate. We were in a little area that had gates at both ends. It was made that way so no dog could accidently slip out and escape.

"Are you Ella and Sophie?" a guy asked. He wasn't much older than us.

"I'm Ella," she replied. "And this is Sophie."

He walked toward us. In his hands were two very small, very cute dogs. They were Maltese—I recognized the breed. They had matching blue ribbons in their fur.

"I'm Ethan," he said.

"Pleased to meet you," I said. "And what are your dogs' names?" I asked as I gave one of them a scratch behind the ears.

"This is Zig and Zag," he said, "But they're not my dogs."

"Are you an international dog thief?" I asked.

"Not quite. I'm a dog walker."

"And you're here to walk them?"

"Actually, Soph, you're here to walk them," Ella said.

"Walking Zig and Zag is my different?"

"Zig and Zag are part of your different," Ella said, and Ethan just smiled.

✣ ✣ ✣

As Ella had promised, Zig and Zag were part of the different—a very small part. There were also a pair of standard poodles named Shadow and Lola, a Doberman named Tilo, two mixed breeds called Grunt and Winnie, a big greyhound named King, two Chihuahuas named Harley and Choncho, and one very large Great Dane called Tiny. I was proud I could handle all the names. Now I had to prove I could handle all the dogs.

The smaller dogs were all attached to me by leashes hooked to a belt around my waist. The bigger ones were on individual leashes. On Ethan's recommendation I went for balance and held the Great Dane and greyhound in my left hand, and the two big poodles and the Doberman in the other. The Doberman wasn't the biggest, but from what I'd been told he was most likely to give me a problem, and I had to keep him on a tight leash—both literally and figuratively.

"Look this way," Ella ordered. "I have to take a few more pictures."

The dogs and I posed for the pictures. I knew that kittens playing pianos, and cute dogs, got retweeted and favored and posted and pinned more than almost anything else. Me with a herd of dogs would generate a lot of interest for me. Maybe I should have worn my Wonder Woman costume if I really wanted to ramp up the score.

Funny, but sometimes I'd wondered how one specific friend and follower was viewing my posts. I knew I shouldn't really care how Luke felt or what he thought of me and what I was doing, but I did. It wasn't so much that I had feelings *for* him as I had feelings *about* him. I guess I wanted to prove him wrong and show him what he was missing out on. I wanted him to see that I could be completely unpredictable.

He, on the other hand, was completely predictable. There were pictures of him with a couple of girls. One of them was a repeating theme. She was pretty but had that "I know I'm hot" look that I hated. He hadn't changed his status from *single*—I knew because I checked every day—but I figured it was only a matter of time. I just couldn't believe that it mattered to me as much as it did.

"Just do it the way I told you," Ethan said, startling me out of my thoughts.

He had given me a little lesson on walking multiple dogs and how to be in charge.

"Remember," Ethan said, "establish dominance."

"I'll try, but they do outweigh me," I said.

"The Great Dane almost outweighs you. Just take it slowly," Ethan said.

"I wasn't planning on racing."

"And remember, you're walking *them*. They're not walking *you*."

"I guess that's still up for debate."

The dogs were already pulling in different directions. The Great Dane was lying down, so he was only creating inertia. There were eleven dogs with eleven minds, and there might be eleven different directions that interested them. I had to at least get them all moving in the same direction to begin with.

"I've been walking most of them for years, so they know the commands," Ethan said.

"Most of them?" I asked.

"Tiny is new, but he's a sweetheart. Take charge!" Ethan barked.

"Sit!" I said. Three of the biggest dogs listened, including Tiny, who got up slightly in order to sit down. "Sit!" I said more firmly, and five of the others did as they were ordered. Zig and Zag just looked at me like I was speaking a foreign language. I figured it didn't matter, though, because once we got going, they'd be pulled along by the bigger dogs.

"Heel!" I commanded, and they all got to their feet and we started walking.

It was reassuring that they were listening. Ethan had said that the secret was letting them know who was in control. Control. I was good at that, and according to my brother and Luke and Ella, I was pretty good at giving orders.

We moved along the path that ringed the park. It was a popular route, people walking, running, riding bikes and walking their dogs. The path wasn't much wider than the dogs extended out on both sides of me. Some people looked at us with amusement. Others appeared annoyed, and some, afraid. Runners and people on bikes tended to move as far off to one side as possible or even bumped up onto the grass. Those with dogs either went really wide around me or, worse, didn't move far enough, and we were in danger of tangling our leashes.

I moved slightly off the path at times, pulling in leashes and giving continual orders and tugs to get the dogs' attention. It was more than a little unnerving to think I had this many dogs. I did quick mental calculation—I had close to five hundred pounds in dogs at the ends of these leashes. I was outweighed by more than three times.

I glanced over my shoulder. Ella and Ethan were trailing behind. We were almost halfway to our destination—the lot where Ethan's van was parked. Once there he'd load the dogs into the vehicle and return them to their homes. I could see the parking lot ahead. This hadn't been bad at all. In fact, it had been fun. I missed having a dog. If I wasn't going away to school, I would have talked to my father about the possibility of us getting another one.

And that's when I saw the squirrel—and so did the dogs.

DAY 54

I seemed to be spending more and more time looking at Twitter, searching my name, responding to posts on my Facebook wall or looking at pictures on Instagram. It was fun to see how people were reacting, and I even took time to answer a lot of them. It seemed only polite. As I gained more friends and followers, it took more and more time. If things continued at this rate, I wouldn't have time to keep doing new things and reporting on them and responding to the reactions. Right now I could still do it, and I really was having fun.

My Twitter and Instagram accounts had about the same number of people—around twelve hundred—but Instagram seemed to generate a lot more interest, more likes and reposts, than the Twitter account did.

I opened up Facebook and scrolled down through my timeline, looking at the comments that had been posted. People were so supportive. They offered suggestions for activities—that was partly how Ella was getting some of her ideas, and she made some of the arrangements through social-media contacts—as well as just cheering me on. It made me feel good to know I wasn't doing this journey alone.

Many people had viewed the dog-walking pictures, and—I saw a comment that wasn't so nice:

So the beautiful, rich girl does a few things that most people would pay to do themselves and somehow we're supposed to think you're some kind of hero. More like a zero or a spoiled brat. Why don't you try to do something that does some good for somebody instead of indulging in your own little fantasies?

I felt like I'd been punched in the stomach. For a second I had the strange thought that it was Luke who'd posted it. Of course it wasn't. It was some random girl. I looked a little at her profile. She seemed to be around my age, and her interests were Oreo cookies, techno-pop and "hanging." Like she was so noble herself.

I needed to speak to Ella, but as I grabbed my phone I realized I had to do something first. I felt my lower lip start to quiver as I started to cry.

* * *

"Look, you can't stop things like that," Ella said. "There are always going to be haters, so you can't take it personally. Haters are gonna hate."

"I guess that's easy for you to say because it wasn't about you."

"Some of us get used to the occasional negative comment. Remember, not everybody in life is going to love you."

"I don't think everybody is going to love me," I protested.

"Then suck it up. You put yourself out there, and somebody is always going to try to knock you down. That's the thing about the Internet—you don't have to be right to have an opinion."

"But the thing is, she *is* right," I said.

"What?"

"She's right."

"You're not a spoiled brat. That's just stupid," Ella said. "And if you don't believe me, then look how other people defended you with their posts after she put that nasty message up."

"I know a lot of people have said nice things about what I was doing, and some were even angry at her post, but still, this has been a pretty selfish summer, if you think about it."

"You're one of the least selfish people I've ever met. You've always been the one to do things for your family, your friends. You were part of the social justice club at school and—"

"And she's still right," I said, cutting Ella off. "It's all pretty indulgent."

"So now you're blaming me?" Ella snapped.

"Of course I'm not blaming you!"

"'Cause I went to a lot of work to arrange things, and instead of being grateful you're angry that I haven't arranged the right—"

"Really, I'm not blaming you," I said.

"That's good, because you really haven't thanked me for what I'm doing."

"I'm really grateful. I'm sure I've said thank you."

"No, you haven't. It's been like you're doing me a favor in doing these things."

"I never thought that!"

"Then show some gratitude. Do you know how hard it's been to arrange some of these things?"

"You've done an amazing job, and I know it hasn't been easy. So really, really, really, thank you, Ella, for all the work you've done and for everything you're going to do."

"Well, you're welcome. It's been my pleasure."

"It's just...I hope you won't mind, but I might want to try to set up a couple of different types of different."

Ella gave me a questioning look. "What do you have in mind?"

"They don't even have to count as official differents if you don't think they should, and you don't have to go with me if you don't want to."

"We're in this together. Besides, somebody has to take the pictures. So what do you have in mind?"

I smiled. "You'll just have to come along and see. You're not the only one who can keep a secret."

❖ ❖ ❖

Today Ella and I spent the afternoon in the kitchen of the Good Shepherd Center, helping to make the evening meal. We peeled and chopped all the ingredients for a beef stew. Not a chunky, new and improved stew from the can, but a really chunky, new and improved stew made with real ingredients. It was also a really, really big stew that was going to feed over a hundred people. It was a lot of work, but the work was well worth it when we got to be part of serving it.

We stood behind a counter, wearing aprons and hairnets, and served each man and woman as they came by. They were people who lived on or close to the streets of the city. Some were homeless, and others were just hanging on by their teeth.

It was strange to think that these people had probably eaten better and had a healthier meal than my father and brother had today. I couldn't write that without my father knowing that's what I was thinking. I also couldn't let myself think that way.

Some of the people were incredibly friendly and thanked us. Others were so shy or wary that they didn't even look our way. Others looked scared or confused. Those were the hardest for me.

Each person got the same serving—a big bowl of hot stew, a freshly baked bun and as much coffee or tea as they could drink. I wondered if this was the only meal some of them were going to have today.

I knew that a whole lot of stories were in the room with us. I assumed most were sad, and some had to be tragic. I guess I can understand why. Still, that didn't stop some people from being grateful for what they had and what they'd been given, even it was only a bowl of stew.

There aren't many homeless people in the suburb where I live. I've never seen one. I think they all end up here in the city. At first I didn't talk to anybody while I was serving. I would like to say that I was trying to respect their privacy, but really I was just a bit confused and scared myself. All of us are afraid of different. Maybe that's been one of the most important lessons I've learned over the summer. Being afraid or unsure or uncertain doesn't mean you shouldn't or couldn't do something.

I started my conversations with small talk when I was helping to give out extra food and cleaning up. Some of them didn't want to have anything to do with me. Others were just so polite and friendly, and somehow happy despite it all. How could anybody be that strong or that brave?

I can't imagine what it would be like not to have a home, to live on the streets. What I know is that this isn't something anybody would ever want to have happen, but sometimes bad things happen that put people out there. One of the people who works at the center told us that being homeless means you're almost always going to be hungry and cold and wet and worried and deprived of sleep. These were homeless people, but they were people. Maybe they weren't that much different from you or me.

I don't want to compare my life to theirs, but on some level I think I get it. There's something about losing a parent that makes you think about losing them both, and that would mean losing your home. Not that I've ever thought my brother and I would end up on the streets. But I've thought we'd have to go and live somewhere else. That's something that's worried me, been part of me, since my mother died.

I went there today because of something that somebody posted on my wall. I want to tell her she was right and thank her. I have been selfish—so selfish that I hadn't even thanked Ella for all the work she was doing. Today was a different different.

Some of the differents I've done I know I'll never do again. I've already signed up here for a shift next week.

DAY 56

We strolled through the lobby of the hotel. We were each in a dress suitable for an evening event, along with appropriate heels and subtle makeup. Of course, I didn't know what we were going to do, but I was actually pleased when Ella described the way we were supposed to dress. How much bad could happen when we were all done up like this?

I'd been careful about what I wore. I wanted to look nice but not too nice. I didn't want to be show-offy in any way. Wherever we were going, I wanted people to look at both of us. Ella looked really good tonight. I wasn't sure if I should say anything or not. If I did compliment her, would she say something like, *You mean better than I usually look?* or *Not as good as you* or something like that? I was thinking about this too much.

I was thinking about everything too much. Sometimes I figured it would be better to just forget about all of this stuff Ella was having me do and lose myself in my textbooks.

Roaming the main hall, we could see that the hotel had almost a dozen banquet halls, and judging from what we'd seen—brides in white dresses and bridesmaids in assorted and sometimes hideous gowns—a number of weddings were going on.

I'd only been to a few weddings in my life, but they always seemed like such happy events. Two people starting a life together with dreams and hopes, living happily ever after. Happily ever after—I guess that worked sometimes.

When I was really little, before my mother died, I used to spend a lot of time looking at my parents' wedding pictures. They were both so young that at first I didn't even know it was them. My mother was in her white gown, and my father in a ridiculous baby-blue tuxedo that he and all the groomsmen wore. Those tuxes were almost as bad as the hideous peach dresses with big puffy sleeves that my mother's bridesmaids all wore and—just then two bridesmaids walked by me, dressed as if they could have been from my parents' wedding! How amazing, how sad, how ugly. I'd read that the bridesmaids are supposed to look bad so the bride looks better. The bride in this wedding would have looked like Miss Universe.

What struck me was how happy everybody looked in my parents' wedding pictures. How happy even the two bridesmaids that had just walked by looked. Weddings were supposed to be about happily ever after, and part of that happy was that they didn't know what the future would hold. It was almost guaranteed to be a mixture of good and bad, happy and sad. What was that line in the vows? *For richer, for poorer, in sickness and in health, until death do us part*. Death did happen. Eventually to everybody. Sooner for some.

"So we have to make a decision," Ella said.

"And that decision is?"

"Which wedding we're going to crash."

No surprise. I'd started to think that was probably the reason we were here—it was the only reason I could think of unless I was being married off.

"You seem pretty calm about this one," Ella said.

"Why shouldn't I be? Minimal chance of death, a survivable level of embarrassment, and you'll be going in with me, correct?"

"How can I take pictures if I'm not right there? It's not like we can ask the wedding photographer to snap a couple of pictures of you—or can we?"

"Probably not. So what are your criteria for deciding which wedding to crash?" I asked.

"I think the bigger, the better."

"That makes sense."

"And we need to blend in. If everybody else is Asian, we'll probably stand out, and we don't want to stand out."

"You've obviously given this a lot of thought," I said.

"I give *all* of these activities a lot of thought."

"And I'm grateful. Have I mentioned that?"

"It never hurts to mention it again. So, next, I want one with a live band that's playing music I like."

"And how does that help us blend in?" I asked.

"It doesn't. I just want a live band—it probably means they've spent more money on the wedding, and more money probably means better food."

"Unless they spent all the money on the band and scrimped on the food," I suggested.

"I hadn't thought of that. Let's start checking them out."

I followed behind Ella as she stopped at the door of each banquet hall and read the sign that listed the event taking place inside. We watched as people went in and out, listened for the music that swelled as doors opened, peeked inside and discussed each possibility. I was quite content to take all the time in the world to walk around and check out each one. The more time we spent out here, doing assessments, the less time we had to spend in one of those rooms.

"I think this is the one," Ella finally said.

"Why this one and not the other four we've looked at?"

"It meets the criteria, plus did you notice the cute guys who just went in there?" She pulled open the door, and the music swelled. "After you."

There had to be close to fifty tables, with eight seats at each table, which added up to a lot of people to hide among. Over to the side, by a crowded dance floor, was an eight-piece band. At the front were the bride and groom, seated with their groomsmen and bridesmaids—altogether there were eighteen of them. I couldn't imagine having that many people in your bridal party. Did anybody really have that many good friends, ones they needed to have in their wedding party? I had Ella and a couple of others, and really, having that many people in a bridal party seemed more like Facebook friends than real friends.

Anxiously I looked around for somebody to stop us, ask us questions, do something, but there was nobody.

"We need to circulate," Ella said. I followed her farther into the room. It felt much safer in the middle than it had at the edges.

"We don't want to sit down until we're sure there's space at a specific table," Ella said.

"I was also thinking we should ask whoever we meet if they're on the bride's side or the groom's side before they can ask us."

"Brilliant! Then we can claim we're with the other side," Ella said.

"Even better, we can say we're the date of somebody on the other side, so we don't even have to know anything about the bride or the groom."

"So smart! So we're nothing more than random plus-ones who don't know anything at all about Sonya and Richard."

"Who are Sonya and Richard?"

"They're the bride and groom. It was on the board. Somebody would be suspicious if you didn't know the names of the bride and groom. Although, Sophie, I am impressed by your level of deviousness around all of this."

"I guess I've been learning from the best."

"Compliments, compliments, compliments."

Ella took my hand and led me onto the dance floor. We squeezed through the couples and took a spot in the middle of the crowd, where there already were half a dozen females—including a couple of bridesmaids—dancing together. We joined in. I loved that girls could do this.

❖ ❖ ❖

We had soft drinks from the bar, sampled the munchies, mingled, danced together and were asked to dance by some guys. I was happy when the first one who came up asked Ella to dance instead of me. We'd made up stories and used fake names—she was Meadow and I was Sky, the reverse of our fast-food names. Those names had just popped out of my mouth when we first introduced ourselves to people, and we stuck with them.

It hadn't taken long for me to get beyond my initial fear of being discovered and simply start enjoying myself. This could become a habit. Where else could you get free food and drink and be part of a big, happy party?

"Could everybody please take a seat!" the master of ceremonies said into the mic.

"No worries," Ella said. "We're going to sit at table thirty-eight."

Each table had a sign indicating its designated number.

"Why thirty-eight?" I asked.

"It's at the back, which means it's populated by the least connected people, and I've been watching, so I'm pretty sure there are vacant seats. If there aren't, we'll just say we're at the wrong table, and if worse comes to worse, just head out to the lobby until people get up and start dancing again."

We joined everybody else shuffling around to get to their seats. It was a slow process as people mingled, talked, laughed and generally continued having a great time. It amused me that more than a few people greeted "Sky and Meadow" by name. We'd already talked to enough people to have new friends. It felt like we belonged, like we *were* friends.

We sat down at two of four empty seats at the table and introduced ourselves. The others were friends of the bride, so we were, obviously, friends of the groom. Two other people joined us, and we exchanged greetings. Thank goodness they were friends of the bride as well, so we threw around Richard's name.

We settled in as the speeches began. They were exactly what I'd expected. The parents of the bride and groom made speeches about when they were little, there was a short video clip and pictures on the screen behind the bridal party, followed by the maid of honor's speech and finally the best man's.

His speech was like the ones I'd heard at weddings I was actually supposed to be at. It was a combination of praise, insults and attempts at humor that didn't quite make it. I didn't understand that whole *guy thing* where someone puts down his best friend in front of his friends, family and family to be. Males were an entirely different species that we interacted with but didn't really understand. I was sure they didn't understand us any better.

After the main speeches a man with a wireless microphone started going through the room, allowing individuals to add their words or congratulations and giving little impromptu speeches.

"You've enjoyed this one," Ella said as she leaned in close, talking over the next speech.

"It's been fun and easy. Are you disappointed that it wasn't difficult or embarrassing enough?"

"Not disappointed at all. You never know how one thing leads to another."

There was polite applause as the little speech ended, and Ella jumped to her feet.

"Over here, over here!" she yelled, waving her hands in the air.

What was she doing? And then I realized. She had gotten the attention of the man with the microphone, and he was coming our way!

"Get ready to give your speech to the bride and groom," Ella said.

I think she expected that I'd be scared or shocked. Instead I got to my feet and grabbed the microphone.

"Sonya and Richard," I said, my voice bouncing around the room. I held the microphone a little farther from my mouth. "I know I haven't known either of you for long, but I can honestly say I've never seen Richard look happier or Sonya look lovelier. I wish you all the happiness and joy you desire and deserve." I picked up a glass from the table. "To the bride and groom!"

Everyone picked up their glasses. "To the bride and groom!" they called out, then clinked glasses and drank a toast.

I sat back down. Ella clinked her glass against mine. "Pretty impressive."

"Don't you remember who won the public-speaking contest in eighth grade?" I asked.

"Still impressive. A toast to you, Sky. You are certainly becoming different!"

DAY 57

I didn't get home until late, and I slept in even later. I'd searched for some shots of Ella and me dancing but couldn't find anything without somebody in the background who would possibly give away where we'd been, and of course I couldn't put up any shots of the bride and groom. Social media made the world a much smaller place, and it was probably best that nobody ever connected Meadow and Sky with Ella and me. Maybe it was pretty cool to crash a wedding, but it wouldn't be so cool for those people to know about it. Richard and Sonya had seemed like really nice people, but I wasn't going to test that niceness. Besides, I didn't want to have our presence take anything away from their day. It needed to be marked by love, not wedding crashers.

It had been such a wonderful wedding that I'd wished I actually did know the bride and groom. They'd looked so happy, and they made such a nice-looking couple. It would have been nice to put a picture of them on Instagram. Then I had another idea.

I rushed off to the living room and pulled open the buffet. Inside were lots of family pictures, including my parents' wedding pictures. I hadn't looked at the pictures in years, but they were still so familiar to me. I started to search, looking for one very specific picture—I could see it in my mind. I went page by page through the album, and then there it was.

It was of my mother and father, each holding a piece of wedding cake that they were about to feed to each other. They both looked so happy, so innocent and so young. And really, they were all of those things.

In that picture my mother was only six years older than I was now. She was two years out of college and three years before she gave birth to me. Almost exactly fourteen years later, she'd died. None of that was fair. Not to her, not to my father, not to me and not to my brother. But what did fairness have to do with anything?

I removed the picture from the little white tabs holding it in place. I photographed it with my phone and posted it. I wanted people to see her and my father on that day and know how happy they'd been. That was what weddings were about. What happened later was beyond anything that anybody could control, and it was better that they didn't know what was coming. No amount of worry, no attempt to control, no hope for predictable, could change some things. They just happened. Control was an illusion. One I was learning not to desperately cling to.

DAY 58

"I loved that picture of your parents' wedding," Ella said as we drove along.

"A lot of people liked it."

It had been retweeted and liked and commented on more than almost anything else I'd posted. Several followers said how much I looked like my mother. My father told me that all the time, but I'd always had trouble seeing it. Of course, it was a compliment. My mother was really pretty, and so kind. I remembered that, but people were always saying it too. She was also brave. Back then I didn't realize just how brave she'd been, the way she'd handled herself at the end.

Ella pulled into a parking lot.

"We're going to a country-and-western bar?"

"Where did you expect we were going dressed like this?"

We were both in checkered shirts, cowboy hats and cowboy boots.

"And how are we going to get into a bar when we're underage?" I asked.

"All covered."

"I guess I should just be grateful you're not bringing me to a rodeo," I said.

"Funny, that's funny. It will get even funnier as this night develops."

Oh, that was bad. "You're not actually going to take me to a rodeo another day, are you?"

"No rodeo, I promise, but if we did go to one, we'd get another opportunity to wear cowboy hats," she said. "I think I look fantastic in a cowboy hat, cowboy boots and boot-cut jeans."

"Where did you even get these hats and boots?"

"It's amazing what connections social can make. The same person who suggested and arranged this different also got us the clothing. Come on."

We walked toward the bar. It was called the Electric Cowboy and featured a gigantic neon image of a cowboy leaning against a fence. The lights changed back and forth to show him taking off his hat. I'd never been to the place, but the sign was sort of a landmark in our city.

Circling around to the front of the bar, I saw there was a big lineup snaking all the way across the front of the building to the door. There must have been a hundred people waiting to get in.

"We're not going to get in for hours," I said.

"We won't have to wait."

Ella walked down the line. I followed along, staying close and trying not to look at the people waiting. I hesitated and then stopped as she detoured around the people at the head of the line. She was getting a lot of nasty looks as she "excused" herself until she was standing right at the door, which was being guarded by a very large, menacing-looking cowboy. He had to be the bouncer. He bent down—way down—to talk to Ella. Did she really think she could talk her way inside? She could be charming, but there was no way—

The big cowboy shot me a smile and gestured for me to come over.

I "excused" my way through the people at the front of the line. I got some glares and some snide remarks that I couldn't make out.

"Soph, this is Stretch," Ella said.

"Pleased to meet you, ma'am," Stretch said. He tipped his hat.

"Glad to meet you as well."

"You two sure 'nough are pretty little fillies," he said in a cowboy drawl.

"Thanks, pardner," Ella offered.

"You look as pretty as on your profiles," he added.

"Our profiles. Do you follow me? Are you a Facebook friend?" I thought I would have remembered a Stretch, but I friended everybody who asked, and the requests just kept coming.

"I am. Nice picture of your parents' wedding."

"Thanks. It's my favorite."

"And it's nice of you to honor them that way. I was starting to think you two weren't going to be coming tonight," he said.

"You knew we were coming?"

"Of course I did, little lady," he said.

"This was all arranged by Stretch," Ella said. "He's the one who contacted me with the idea and even got us the clothes."

"That was so kind of you." I probably should have waited to say that until I knew what he had arranged.

"It's my pleasure," he said and gave a little bow.

"I really like your accent," Ella said. "Where are you from?"

"New Jersey."

"New Jersey?" Ella and I both asked in unison.

"The Jersey Shore."

"But your accent," I said. "You sound like you're from somewhere down south."

"The Jersey Shore is the *south* part of the state," he said, suddenly speaking in a clear Jersey accent. "My name is Tony "Stretch" Greco, so my background is even farther south, in Italy. You girls never heard of a spaghetti western?"

Ella and I both burst into laughter, and he flashed a gigantic smile.

"Now I want you to remember our deal," Stretch said.

"What deal?" I asked.

"Because we're underage, they had to make special arrangements for us to be here, and we have to promise not to order alcoholic drinks," Ella explained.

I turned to Stretch. "Believe me, that's the last thing I'd do."

"Good. You go on inside, and I'll get another bouncer to work the door so I can join you in a while," he said, switching back to his cowboy twang. He held the door open for us, and a swell of sound from a steel guitar came flowing out.

"How come they get to go in first?" some guy yelled out from behind us in the line.

I cringed as we all turned around.

"We've been waiting a long time," the man yelled, and his buddy nodded.

"And you're gonna be waiting a whole lot longer, partner," Stretch drawled, "'cause where I come from, we treat women with a little more respect."

Not in any of the reality TV episodes I'd seen, but I didn't say that.

The guy made another negative comment, and Stretch let go of the door and walked toward him. Ella grabbed my arm and pulled me inside. The door shut behind us before we could see what was going to happen, and the country music enveloped us.

The place was just packed. We weaved through the tables and chairs and the people standing four deep at the bar. It was a sea of cowboy hats, cowboy boots, jeans, checkered shirts and women with big hair and tight skimpy tops. I felt over-dressed and under-haired.

The music was really loud. I'd never been a real fan of the music part of country music, but I found the words interesting. They always seemed to tell a story. It might be a story about going to prison, or a cheatin' man, or a pickup truck breaking down, or a girlfriend who left the guy, but there was always a story.

I remembered a joke I'd once heard, that if you play a country song backward, you get back your girlfriend, your dog is no longer dead, and your brother is released from prison.

There were a lot of smiles and friendly conversations and hooting and hollering. We stopped at the edge of the dance floor. It was crammed with people doing a complicated, coordinated line dance. I'd seen it done on TV and in movies, and it did look like fun. If learning to line-dance was the different for tonight, then the scariest thing that could happen was some guy in cowboy boots putting his heel down on my toes.

"Is line dancing the different?"

"I didn't bring you here for that. Your different is on the other side of the dance floor."

I looked through the dancers. There was a big red rubber thing. It looked like an inflatable swimming pool. Was I supposed to go swimming—no, wait, didn't they do mud wrestling at bars like this? That would be awful, terrible, embarrassing. And then I saw what was in the middle of the "pool," and I suddenly thought that mud wrestling wouldn't have been that bad.

❖ ❖ ❖

Stretch—Tony—walked awkwardly across the circular arena, his feet sinking into the soft rubber surface. Thank goodness it was soft.

"You ready?" he asked.

"As ready as I'm ever going to be," I said from my perch atop the mechanical bull.

"So this is your first time, right?"

"First time."

"There's nothing to it. Hardly anybody gets hurt."

"Hardly anybody?"

He shrugged. "An occasional sprain, a couple of separated shoulders—there's only been one broken wrist that I can remember in all the years we've had it."

"I guess that's reassuring."

"It'll start slowly, a little bit of spinning and a bit of bucking, but nothing to worry about. Do you have a tight grip?"

I nodded. I'd wrapped the little rope around my hand so tightly that it was starting to cut off the circulation in my fingers.

"Use your free hand and arm as a counterweight. Throw it back as you get thrown forward. You're gonna end up with a fair crowd," Stretch said. "People like to watch a pretty girl up here."

It didn't really matter much to me. Eventually my audience was going to be a lot bigger than the people surrounding the ring. Ella would be taking pictures for me to put up.

"Okay, let me get out of here, and you can signal the man at the controls to start," Stretch said. "Who knows? You could be a real bull rider."

That was not exactly how I'd ever thought of myself. I just felt scared and exposed and worried that I'd embarrass or hurt myself in front of everybody.

Stretch bounced away across the rubberized floor, leaving me alone in the middle of the ring. Well, me and the mechanical bull. It was brown and black, with big, pointy horns. They looked sharp and painful.

I gave the signal to start.

The bull started vibrating and humming, and then it began moving. It did a little dip, then a little bit of a turn. It started to go faster. More dips, more spins and more abrupt changes in direction. But still nothing I couldn't withstand. I had thought this was going to be much worse.

People surrounding the ring started to clap and cheer. I caught a quick glimpse of Ella, who was front row, her cowboy hat in hand, waving it and whooping for me. She wasn't the only one. Like Stretch had predicted, a crowd was gathering. Part of me would have preferred to be completely alone, but another part liked the idea of people watching me successfully ride the bull. I wasn't doing badly for a "little filly."

The bull spun around again, faster, and I caught another quick glimpse of Ella. Then she disappeared as I twirled away. I couldn't even try to look at her anymore. I had to focus on the bull. It spun around quickly, jerking me a bit to the side, and for a split second I thought I was going to be thrown before I regained my balance. The bull picked up steam, dipping, spinning and bucking all at once. I threw my arm back as I was bucked forward, trying desperately to hold on with my legs as I felt myself rising up into the air, and then there was another jerk, and I was flying through the air!

Everything seemed to slow down as I soared upward, spinning, the crowd roaring in reaction, and then hit the rubber floor face first. I tried to push myself up, but before I could do anything I was pulled to my feet by strong hands. It was Stretch, and Ella was with him.

"Are you all right?" Ella asked.

"I'm fine…good." I turned to Stretch. "Was that a good ride? Did I last very long?"

"You done good!"

"Can I go again?"

"You don't have to," Ella said. "Your different is done."

"I don't have to. I want to. So can I try it again, Stretch?"

"You can ride that bull another half a dozen times, if you want."

"I think a couple more would be nice." I paused. "And then Ella's climbing aboard, right?"

"Count me in."

❖ ❖ ❖

The pictures had generated a lot of likes and comments. My absolute favorite was Ella and me posed on the bull together, waving our cowboy hats. I'd also posted pictures of us on the dance floor. Those were favorites too.

After riding the bull we'd learned how to line-dance. I found out that line dancing didn't just *look* like fun but *was* fun. We spent almost the whole night out there, dancing along with everybody else. When we made mistakes—and we made many of them—we were just offered help and encouragement. I'd found out that cowboys and cowgirls were just about the most friendly and nice people in the world. I'd also found out that almost none of them lived on farms or were from the country. They were just people like Ella and me. We'd decided we'd go back to dance again—Stretch said he'd get us another special invitation. I might just get back up on that bull as well.

It was a great night, and it made for three new differents—cowboy nightclub, bull riding and line dancing. I was on a roll of different.

DAY 59

"I'm just glad it isn't broken," my father said.

"So am I. The doctor said it's just a sprained wrist, and not even a bad one. He said I just have to leave it in the sling for a day or two and it will be fine. And thanks for getting me."

"It's no problem. It's not the first time I've had to go to the emergency department for one of my children, and it probably won't be the last."

"Ella drove me, but she had to go. She had a date," I explained.

"I thought you two were taking a summer vacation from boys."

"Only I am."

"I knew you two were going to a rock-climbing gym, but what happened?"

"I did a little rock falling. I was halfway up the wall, and I slipped."

"Weren't you wearing a harness?"

"I was harnessed, and I was wearing a helmet. I didn't fall. I lost my grip and swung forward and banged into the wall hard on my wrist. Not hard enough to break, thank goodness, but hard enough to hurt."

The instructor had said I'd "frozen," and that was what had gotten me in trouble. I *had* frozen, but he could have at least said he was sorry or tried to be nicer about it. It was like he was angry with me for getting hurt.

Ella hadn't been much better. We'd tried to get hold of my father, but when we couldn't reach him, she had to take me to the hospital. She said she was tight for time, so she dropped me off at the ER and then went home to get ready for her date. I don't think I would have just left her even if I had a date.

"I guess we should at least be grateful that it's your left wrist," he said.

We pulled into the driveway, and Oliver was waiting at the front door. He came running down the drive and was at my side almost before I could get out of the car.

"Are you okay?" he asked. He sounded worried.

"Just a sprained wrist."

"So you didn't break your crown?" he asked.

"My crown? What does that mean?"

"That's what Ella tweeted. That you broke your crown."

Had she really tweeted that? I reached into my purse and pulled out my phone. I'd turned it off in the hospital like the signs said to do and hadn't turned it back on. I pushed the button, and the phone came to life with a rapid series of pings, bongs and red symbols and numbers. I had dozens, no hundreds, of notifications from Twitter, Facebook and Instagram. I did a quick scroll. People were concerned, asking if I was all right and how badly I'd been hurt.

Ella had posted a picture, and it had been retweeted and re-Instagrammed dozens of times. It showed me on the gym floor, holding my wrist, the instructor standing over me. He looked angry, and I looked like I was about to cry. Under the picture was a caption—**The princess fell down and broke her crown.** Why would Ella say something like that? I felt more like crying now than I had when I got hurt.

⁘ ⁘ ⁘

My father had asked me to take some time and think things through before I called Ella. So I had waited, sitting alone in my room, trying to make sense of it all. I'd had time to look through all the notifications and even answer some of the comments. It was slower with only one good hand. People were mostly kind and supportive and worried about me. Ella hadn't been any of those things. She hadn't called or even texted to see if I was all right. It was time to contact her.

I hit her name, the phone dialed, and it started ringing. What was I going to say to her? It rang, but she didn't answer. Maybe it was buried in her purse or had run out of power. Or was she just ignoring me? I sent her a text.

Can we talk?

I waited for a reply. If her phone was dead or tucked away, she wouldn't hear the sound of an incoming text either.

I figured I'd just have to wait. There was a *ping*. It could have been a message from anybody. It was a reply from Ella.

Busy. Talk tomorrow. Hope your wrist is good.

I guessed it would have to wait until the next day. Right now the part of me that hurt the most wasn't my wrist.

DAY 60

Ella bounced into my room like nothing was wrong. Maybe nothing *was* wrong. No, just because *she* was happy about everything didn't mean that *I* was happy.

"So how's the wrist?"

"Sprained."

"But not broken?"

"No, only a sprain."

"The instructor told you it wasn't broken. *I* told you it wasn't broken. You should have listened to Dr. Ella, and you wouldn't have had to go and waste your time at the hospital."

"I wanted to hear it from a doctor instead of you and the rock-climber guy."

She shook her head. "How predictable—you need to have everything checked out. The doctor probably told you what a wonderful patient you were."

"Excuse me if I wanted to know I was all right. And what do you mean, *a wonderful patient*?"

"You probably waited patiently in the waiting room, did what you were told, said please and thank you to the nurses and doctors. You know what I mean."

"What did you expect me to do, throw furniture at people, swear at the doctor and punch a nurse?"

"That would have at least been interesting and would have made for a tweet worthy of being retweeted."

My head was spinning, but I had my intro. I just had to say what was on my mind and—

"And are you angry about the tweet I put up?" she asked. "Some people who read it said I was being insensitive. I was just making a joke. Maybe it wasn't a good joke, but really, come on, are you going to be upset about that?"

"It's just that it felt like you were laughing at me."

"It wasn't like you were really hurt."

"I *was* hurt, and when you took the picture, when you tweeted it, you didn't know my wrist wasn't broken."

"Even if it was broken, come on—people break things."

"I've never broken anything."

"That is rather regal, don't you think?"

"Regal, like calling me a princess?"

"You shouldn't take things so seriously. We both know that."

"I guess I do."

"Part of your doing differents is being able to realize you don't have to be the best. You don't have to always be up on a pedestal, up there on your throne."

"Throne? The place where a princess would sit?"

"The fact that you're bringing this up at all does make you look like a princess. You know, Sophie, the world doesn't revolve around you."

"What?"

"Everything isn't about you."

"I never said it was."

"You never said it, but that's the way you act. For example, did you even think to ask how my date went last night?"

"I was going to."

"Then go ahead. Ask me."

"Um, how was your date?"

"It was awful, terrible. He is a big cowboy jerk."

"It was somebody we met at the western bar?"

"It was Stretch, and he tried to show me how little respect South Jersey cowboys really have for women."

"I'm so sorry."

"Sorry that he didn't ask you out instead of me?"

"Of course not. Sorry that it didn't work out."

"I would have rather had a sprained wrist and sat in the Emergency department, where some young and handsome doctor probably asked to kiss your wrist to make it better for you."

"What?"

"Not all of us have a charmed life," she said. "Not all of us have everything go right for us all the time."

"Things go wrong for me," I protested.

"Like spraining a wrist? Like Luke breaking up with you?"

"No, more than that."

"What? What went wrong for you?"

I knew what I wanted to say, but I didn't know if I could say it. I started to work it around in my head, and—

"See? You can't even think of anything," she said. "I'm gone."

Ella stormed out of the room. I stood there stunned. I unfroze and stumbled down the stairs just in time to hear the front door slam. I ran out to the porch, but by the time I got there she was already in her car.

"Ella!"

Either she didn't hear me or didn't want to hear me. She squealed away, leaving behind a spray of rocks, the smell of rubber and me. *Now what? Now what?*

❖ ❖ ❖

It took all day and a long discussion with my father to help me work things out. He came up to my room after supper, and I burst into tears. I'd already cried a lot, so I was surprised there were still tears to come out. After I was through crying, we talked. Mostly he listened, which is what I really needed. In the end we decided—*I* decided—that I needed to call Ella again. She hadn't answered when I'd called her right after she drove off, but I had to hope she had calmed down too.

Before I called I had one other thing to do. My iPad was ready, my blog page open, ready for me to write.

Today's different was painful. Much more than spraining a wrist. And by the way, thanks for all the kind comments. It's just a sprain. When it happened, Ella told me it wasn't broken. She was right. She's right almost all the time.

Ella is the best friend I've ever had. The best friend I'm ever going to have. She's been there with me every day since seventh grade. And never more than during the past sixty days. Today was the two-thirds mark of my ninety days of different. I wasn't looking for a cake and candles and presents. I also wasn't looking for the biggest fight of my life with my best friend.

Let me tell you about Ella. She's funny and quirky and brave and strong. She talks too loud and too fast and has an opinion on everything. And most of the time her opinion is right, even when she changes it seven times. If I live to be 125—and from what I've been told sometimes I act like I'm nearly that old—I will never, ever find another friend like her. Today we got into a fight. Friends fight. Friends also make up. I miss you.

With love,

The former princess Sophie

DAY 61

I walked down the concrete stairs to the basement. With each step the acrid smell got stronger. I wouldn't have even known what the smell was if Todd—Officer Todd—hadn't told me. He was behind me, as he was the one who'd contacted Ella before our fight and arranged this different. It probably wasn't a good sign that she hadn't called to come along and take pictures.

I still hadn't heard from her at all. I'd posted my blog late the night before, and it was just after seven thirty in the morning now, earlier than she usually got up, so maybe she hadn't seen it yet. Or maybe she'd seen it and was thinking about how to respond. Maybe she just wasn't going to respond.

"I was a little worried that after your fight with Ella you'd be too upset to come," Todd said.

"Oh yeah, I guess you'd know about that."

"Everybody who follows you knows about that. Has she replied yet?"

"Not yet."

"Don't sweat it. Friends have fights. My best friend and I got into a real bad one once."

"And it all worked out in the end," I said.

He made a strange face. "Well, actually it was never the same between us, and then I moved here and joined the force. We talk—sometimes." He must have seen the look of shock on my face. "But it's different with girls, right? Guys are such chowderheads about relationships. I'm sure it'll be okay. So are you excited about today?"

"I guess I'm more scared than anything." I was also distracted and worried. What if Ella didn't call me, never called me again?

"You certainly sounded scared when I called you the other day."

He'd called just before we went rock climbing, and I *had* been scared. Out of the blue I'd gotten a call from a police officer, and my instant response was that I was in trouble—either they'd changed their minds about not charging us with vandalism or they'd heard we'd crashed a wedding, which was sort of theft of food, or impersonation or something, wasn't it?

"I wasn't scared, just sort of surprised. I hadn't expected you to call."

"I can understand how it could have seemed a bit creepy at first," he said.

"Not creepy. Just surprising."

"So Ella didn't tell you I was going to call?" he asked.

"No, she never lets me know what's coming up, so that I'm not so worried."

"This time you would have been less worried if you'd expected my call." He paused. "She'll call you, I'm sure of it."

"Thanks for saying that."

"Anyway, Ella tweeted that she was looking for somebody who could arrange to take you to a rifle range, so I volunteered," he said.

"Thanks for doing this."

"It's my pleasure. Besides, I go to the range all the time. Like Sarge mentioned, we don't use our weapons very often, and they like us to stay qualified."

"Of course. That makes perfect sense."

We came to a locked door with a small open panel in the middle. A man peeked through the opening, and Todd showed his identification. The door opened and the man welcomed us inside. The smell got stronger.

The place was like something out of a movie. There was a series of long spaces, kind of like lanes in a bowling alley, except at the end of each one, instead of pins, there were targets, outlines of men with concentric circles on the torso.

"You're in firing position number four," said the man who let us in.

We walked over to the lane and stopped in front of a low barrier that was both a table and a wall to stop anybody from wandering closer to the targets. It really did remind me of a bowling alley, which was reassuring and disturbing all at once.

Todd took the metal case he'd been carrying and placed it on top of the counter. He twirled a little combination lock on the side of the case and opened it up to reveal a pistol resting in a sort of foam-filled holder.

"Say hello to my little friend," he said.

"What?"

"It's a line from one of my favorite movies, *Scarface*."

"I've never seen it."

"That's hard to believe. It's a classic. It stars Al Pacino and Michelle Pfeiffer. Say, has anybody ever told you that you look like a young Michelle Pfeiffer?"

I shook my head. "Sorry, I don't know her either."

"Well, believe me, that movie is a classic. As is this gun."

He removed the gun from the case. "This is a Glock 22 Generation 4, albeit a very new version of a classic." He cradled it in his hands. "Isn't it beautiful?"

"Um, yeah, I guess that isn't how I'd describe it."

"Here, take it," he said as he offered it to me.

I pulled slightly away.

"Don't worry. It's not loaded." He pulled some slide thing. "See, no rounds in the chamber and no magazine in the gun." He turned it over and I could see that the handle was sort of hollow-looking.

I took it. It was cold to the touch. "It's heavier than I expected."

"It's twenty-two ounces without a magazine."

"What exactly is a magazine?"

"The bullets are held in a magazine, which some people incorrectly call a clip." He pulled what I assumed was a magazine out of the case. One of the bullets was visible at the end. "It uses .40-caliber ammunition, and it can handle magazines of either fifteen or twenty-two rounds. I prefer twenty-two rounds.

"This is the standard sidearm issued to over 85 percent of the police forces in the country. It is favored because it's highly reliable, resistant to jamming, smooth firing and easily reloaded by simply ejecting one magazine and inserting another."

I nodded like I understood what he meant.

"It has fixed sights, a modified slide frame and a ported barrel to reduce muzzle climb."

"Okay, I'm not sure what any of that means," I finally admitted.

"Rather than tell you, I'll show you."

He took the gun from me and slipped the magazine into the bottom with a click.

"Even now it is still completely safe," he said.

"Does it have a safety?" I asked, thinking about the sort of thing I had heard on TV police shows.

"Technically it's not a safety so much as a safety feature. You see this little blade in the middle of the trigger?" he said as he showed it to me. "You have to firmly place your finger on the center of the trigger, on the blade, to fire it. Now put on your ear protection."

I put on what was basically a set of headphones without music attached—and Todd did the same. He took up a position, holding the pistol in his right hand, steadying it with his left hand, and braced himself.

He fired, and I jumped slightly as bullet after bullet smashed into the target at the end of the lane. The shots were loud, even with our ear protection, and the acrid smell filled the air. There were five or six holes in the target, all clustered around the center in the middle of the figure.

He placed the gun on the counter. "Your sprained wrist. Is it good enough for this?"

"It's my left one that I sprained, and really, it's fine now."

"Good, because you will need both hands. Come here."

Hesitantly I moved closer.

"Pick it up, and don't be afraid—it won't bite you."

Biting wasn't what I was afraid of. Carefully I took the gun in my right hand. My hand was sweaty. Todd came up behind me and reached over me so that his hand was on top of mine and he was right behind me. I felt a little nervous, and at least part of that was from him being so close.

"Now place your second hand on the wrist of your right hand to steady it."

I did as I was told. I felt a little twinge of ache in my wrist.

"Now bring the gun up and look down the sights with your dominant eye to the target. Can you see it?"

"Yes."

"There will be some recoil as you fire. The gun will push back. And there will also be some upward pressure. That's what muzzle climb is. You have to hold the gun firmly to avoid that, or each successive shot will be higher and higher until you're shooting at the sky."

"I'll try to hold it."

"Now take a deep breath, hold your breath, and gently press your finger against the trigger."

I took a breath and then squeezed the trigger. I was shocked by the pushback and the push up, despite Todd's hand helping to hold it firm.

"Very good!" he yelled. "You hit the target!"

I'd hit the very top of the target, well above the outlined figure.

"Now you can try it on your own," he said.

He released his hold on my hand and backed away. I felt both relieved and less safe.

"Go ahead," he said. "But this time I want you to fire off the rest of the magazine. Go for it."

I thought through everything Todd had said. I brought the pistol up, aimed at the target, squeezed my finger and fired, then fired again and again and again. With each shot I worked to keep the gun level, but I could see the shots hitting the target slightly higher each time. I pulled the trigger again, and there was nothing. Was the magazine empty?

Todd came and took the gun from me. He pulled off his ear protection, and I did the same.

"You did very well," he said.

"I guess I had a good teacher."

"Now that you've fired a gun, you might appreciate *Scarface*."

"I'll try to see it," I said.

"Do you want to see it with me?"

"Are you asking me out?"

He looked embarrassed, and I suddenly felt bad for making him feel bad.

"I'm sorry. I guess I shouldn't have said that. I wasn't trying to make you uncomfortable," he said.

"It's just that I'm really not seeing anybody. I had sort of a bad breakup, and I'm trying not to date anybody right now, not for the entire summer. It's sort of one of my differents."

"I understand. Been there and done that. You are eighteen, right?" he asked.

"My birthday was in May. On the twentieth."

"Mine's May 17!" Todd said. "We're both Taurus—although I was born four years before you."

"You're twenty-two? I thought you were older."

"It's the uniform. Being a cop makes people think you're

older. It's only sort of creepy, my being twenty-two and asking out an eighteen-year-old. If I was twenty-five or you were seventeen, it would be definitely higher on the creep scale."

"It's not creepy. It's a nice compliment. It's just like I said though. I'm not really dating at all right now."

"In a year or so, if you decide you might want to see that movie *Scarface* with me, well, you have my email and phone number. No pressure, no expectations."

"Thanks."

"You can also call if you need to talk," he said. "If Ella doesn't call and you need to talk to somebody about it."

I let out a big sigh.

"Good friends shouldn't let a fight get in the way of their friendship, especially one as good as yours. She'll call."

"Again, thanks. I appreciate the support."

"Consider it part of our police motto—to serve and protect."

"I guess that would be a little of both."

"And the asking-you-out part...sort of forget about that, especially for now. It's just that you seem older than eighteen."

"I get that all the time. I'm supposed to be like everybody's big sister or mother," I said.

"I don't see you quite that way, but I do like the fact that you're out there, taking risks, doing really interesting things."

"I'm trying, and again, thanks for doing this. And for asking me out."

⁂ ⁂ ⁂

The target was hanging on my bedroom wall. It had really impressed my brother. I hadn't told him that the holes closest to the center of the target had all been made by Todd. Those were the ones that caused him to feel both respect and maybe a little bit of fear of me.

I was trying to think about what I was going to write on my blog. It had been such a strange experience. Maybe stranger than firing the gun was Todd asking me out. One I'd write about on my blog. The other I'd only think about. It was flattering, but like I'd told Todd, I wasn't going to date anybody right now. I was enjoying being single—at least for the summer. When school started I might feel different.

The door opened. "Ella," I gasped.

I rushed to her, and we both burst into tears as we hugged. Somehow the hugging not only made me feel better but also squeezed out more tears. I tried to talk and she tried to talk, but neither of us could form words. Maybe best friends didn't always need words.

DAY 63

We went into the club. I'd never been here before and didn't know what it was about. Going to a club couldn't be the different, because I had been to clubs before and not that long ago. I usually didn't like that sort of thing, although the country bar had been fun. I was a little sad we weren't going back there again, but Ella had made it pretty clear she never wanted to see Stretch again, and I understood that.

Besides, all that mattered was that Ella and I were doing this together. The day before, we'd just hung out. We hadn't talked much, but everything had seemed to be okay.

We walked through the front door, and I could hear music and *really* bad singing. I recognized the song, but it definitely wasn't Adele singing it. It was painfully bad. We walked down a corridor and into the main room, where a woman onstage was singing along to recorded music. Karaoke. She was off key, off tempo and mispronouncing some words, but full-on enthusiastic.

The song soared to a place where Adele would be belting out a high note, and the woman ventured onward and upward without fear or, from what I could tell, any musical training or ability. The song came to an end, mercifully, and there was a smattering of applause from the room and a wild standing ovation from one table.

Either the people at that table were tone deaf and had an unnatural hatred of Adele, or they were the woman's friends. When everybody at the table hugged her and she sat down with them, I knew which it was.

"That was so beyond bad," Ella said. "Which, ironically, makes it even better for you."

"Am I here to do karaoke?"

"You're not going to wait tables."

"But you know I can't sing."

"Everybody can sing. I've heard you sing."

"If you've heard me sing, then you know I'm terrible!"

"No, that woman was terrible. You're just not very good," Ella said.

The MC called out the name of the next singers. Two guys bounced up onto the stage. They were older and balding and had big beer bellies. They were either very happy or very intoxicated—or both.

The music started, and I recognized the tune—"I Love Rock-n-Roll." My father often played it in the car and sang along at the top of his lungs. He was a terrible singer, and unfortunately, while some people thought I looked like my mother, I sang like my father. The two men started to sing. One was actually not bad, which made it even worse for his friend, who was as bad as the imitation Adele.

"Go have a seat, and I'll put your name on the list to sing," Ella said.

"Ella, I really, really don't want to do this."

"I know you don't."

"I'm just not comfortable being up there," I said, pointing to the stage.

"You're *not* comfortable because you're *not* that good."

"So you want me to look silly?" I regretted saying it as soon as the words popped out of my mouth. We were okay, but maybe not that okay.

"I'll admit that's what makes it at least a little funny for me, but we're talking about you. You need to be able to do things you're not good at, that you're even really bad at, and realize that nobody dies."

"I know I'm not going to die up there unless it's dying of embarrassment."

"Nobody has ever died of embarrassment," she said.

"But I'm sure there are people who wanted to."

"Remember, being bad at something doesn't make *you* bad. It just makes you human."

I understood what she meant, but I didn't like being unable to do something well.

"On the bright side, I'm probably not going to sprain a wrist," I said.

"That probably depends on how you hold the microphone. Look at the playlist and choose your song while I go and put your name on the list to perform."

She bounced away before I could say anything else. There was nothing to do but take a seat and try to find a song I wouldn't completely butcher.

* * *

Person after person took to the stage and sang along to the recorded music. I wasn't shocked at just how many people actually wanted to do this but by the wide range of singing ability. Some were plain awful, but others were, well, amazing. Forget *American Idol* and *The Voice*— the most talented singers in the country seemed to be right here in this bar. I had to hope that either I didn't have to follow one of the good ones or that I wouldn't be called at all. Sometimes small improbable hope was better than no hope. I tried to focus on what Ella had said. I wasn't going to die up there on the stage.

"So you haven't told me what your song is going to be," Ella said.

"It's this one right here," I said, pointing down at the play-list. "'Summer Nights' from *Grease*."

"But that's a duet."

"That could be a problem." I paused. "Or maybe I could find somebody to sing the other part. I was hoping I wouldn't have to leave this table to find that person."

"So you want me to sing a love duet with you?" she asked.

"Why not? It wouldn't be any stranger than those two guys who sang the Elton John duet together."

Two men had sung "Don't Go Breaking My Heart" and actually done a remarkably good job. They'd gotten the biggest round of applause of the night.

"So if I do this, do I get to be Sandy or Danny?" Ella asked.

"You can sing whichever part you want. So will you do it?"

She didn't answer.

The singer onstage ended his song, and we clapped along with everybody else. He had been less than good, which made him a good person to follow.

The MC came onto the stage. "And next up is Sophie… Sophie, come on up!"

My heart rose into my throat. I turned to Ella. "Well?"

She smiled. "Just call me Danny."

⁂

In the end, we'd done two songs. It wasn't that we were so good on the first but that we were having fun. Maybe my singing *with* somebody had been cheating, but still, I had sung two songs, and that was sort of the equivalent of one done solo.

I started singing to myself. "*Summer lovin', had me a blast…*"

DAY 64

I turned over and looked at the clock. I was surprised but not surprised to see that it was almost twelve thirty. We had stayed at the karaoke place until late the night before, and then I'd done all the media posting and publishing, but I'd still been unable to get to sleep right away. It had actually been a high getting onstage and making a fool of myself. Ella was right—it wasn't bad to be that bad at something, and being bad together had made it even better.

I started to roll back over, then caught the scent of something cooking—no, something burning. My father must have been trying to make lunch. It was so much easier when they ordered in, but he was trying—and failing—to cook them meals. I couldn't let myself think about that. It had to be their problem, not mine.

The smell was getting stronger.

I climbed out of bed and headed for the kitchen.

Whatever he'd cooked had burned badly, and there was smoke drifting up the stairs!

"Dad! Oliver!" I screamed.

I raced down the hall—a trail of black smoke was snaking along the ceiling. There was a pot on the stove, and flames were licking up its sides and soaring halfway to the ceiling.

I stumbled forward, turned on the tap to get water, then thought better of that. I pulled open the cupboard underneath the sink, knocked things out of the way and grabbed the red fire extinguisher.

I aimed it at the fire, which was getting bigger by the second, and tried to press the handle, but nothing happened. I scanned it and saw a pin holding it up. I pulled the pin and squeezed the handle again. A spray of thick white foam shot out all over the pot and the stove and the wall and the fire. Almost instantly the flames vanished. The fire was gone, smothered. I kept pressing until the entire top of the stove had disappeared beneath the foam. The fire was out.

There was foam everywhere. It reminded me of the soap suds that had filled the room. What was different was the smell. The room was filled with the bitter odor of smoke, which still drifted in a cloud by the ceiling. The wall beside the stove was blackened, stained with smoke and charred by the flames themselves.

"Sophie?"

I turned to see my father and brother standing at the kitchen door. They both looked completely stunned.

"What happened?" my father asked.

"What happened is that you put something on the stove and then you left it."

"We were playing catch," he stammered. He held up the baseball glove on his hand like he was offering proof.

"And you almost burned the house down."

"We were only gone a few minutes," Oliver said.

"It only took a few minutes."

"Thank goodness you were here," my father said.

I walked over and handed him the fire extinguisher. "And if I hadn't been here, if I'd been away at college? You know what would have happened? You would have burned the house down because you were too busy playing catch outside to watch the stove."

"It was an accident. It won't happen again," he said.

"I'm surprised it happened the first time, because you hardly ever cook to begin with. You keep telling me you can take care of things, that you and Oliver can get by without me, but is that really true?" I demanded.

"I'm trying."

"Trying would be having groceries in the house, fixing a meal or two with real ingredients, doing some chores so it doesn't look like the place should be condemned."

"I'm doing the best I can," he said.

"No you're not!" I snapped. He looked as shocked by my words as I felt, but I couldn't stop now. "All you're doing is showing me that I *can't* leave to go away to college because the two of you will either starve to death or burn down the house. Maybe we have to stop pretending that you can do it."

"I can do it," he said. He didn't sound very convinced or convincing.

"Can you? Can you really act like a parent?"

"Come on, Soph, that isn't fair," he said.

"*Fair*? Fair would be that my mother hadn't died or that my father acted like a father and I didn't have to be the one who—" I stopped myself. My father looked like I'd wounded him. I burst into tears and ran from the room.

❖ ❖ ❖

I sensed I wasn't alone. I opened my eyes and rolled over. My father was standing in my bedroom door. He looked as sad as I felt. He looked like he'd been crying. I'd been crying a lot.

"May I come in?" he asked.

I nodded my head weakly.

He came over and sat on the edge of the bed. "It's all cleaned up."

Again I nodded.

"It could have been so much worse if you hadn't found it. I'm so sorry for putting you through all of that," he said.

"I'm sorry too."

"Sorry for what?"

"For the things I said." I was on the verge of tears again.

"You should never be sorry for telling the truth. I let you down. I keep letting you down."

"No, you don't. It's just that—"

"It's just that I need to grow up and be the parent you and Oliver need. You're going away to school and—"

"I don't have to go away."

"Yes, you do. If you don't go away, I'll never forgive myself. I'll do better. I *have* to do better. I'll show you. I promise."

I threw my arms around him, and he hugged me back.

"Could I ask you a question?" he asked.

"Of course."

"Did you ever wonder what it would have been like if it had been the other way around?"

"I don't know what you mean," I said—but I thought I did.

"What it would have been like if your mother had been the one to live?"

And he'd been the one to die.

"I've never thought of that," I said, hoping my lie was convincing.

"I have," he said. "I know it would have been better for Oliver and you."

"Don't say that."

"Your mother was the strong one. She would have been a better parent and..." He let the words trail off.

"We got by," I said.

"And we'll get by when you're gone," he said. "I promise."

DAY 66

The first thing I did was post the pictures. Ella and I looked pretty cool in our get-ups. There had already been a bunch of likes. The pictures did make me smile. Now I just needed to post something more to explain the pictures.

I started typing and then stopped. I put a hand against a bruise on my arm. It was tender to the touch. I was closer when it hit and it really stung. On the bright side, the bruises were the only things left on my skin that were a different color. It had taken a lot of scrubbing, but I'd managed to get rid of the last of the blue and red paint. Each bruise, and each patch of paint that had been on my skin or clothes, was a place where I'd been shot with a paintball. Who would have thought a little plastic ball filled with paint could hurt so much?

We spent the day at a place called Balls of Duty Paintball. *I thought the name was a little hokey—playing off the video game Call of Duty—but once I got there I changed my mind. It was a gigantic indoor facility, and walking around it, I actually felt like I was in the video game. It looked like we were in a run-down city neighborhood of partially destroyed houses and storefronts, with burned-out cars littering the streets. Even though I knew it was all fake, just a big stage really, it was unnerving.*

Somehow I'd thought that my having learned to shoot a real gun would give me an advantage. I was feeling confident. I was so wrong.

I got the first hints of what was coming while we were in the lounge, waiting for our turn to get out there. That's where we met our teammates. They were a bunch of guys in their twenties and early thirties who called themselves the Paintball Wizards. Ella had already sort of met them on the Internet when they approached her and offered to take us paintballing.

They were all dressed in identical black outfits with matching goggles for eye protection. They'd brought the same goggles for us, and that was when I noticed that their outfits had padded chests and legs. There could only be one reason padding was needed. We certainly weren't dressed like them—we'd worn our yoga pants and tops.

It turned out these guys had been doing this for years, on at least one weekend every month and some weekday evenings. They'd fired thousands and thousands of paintball rounds while my whole experience was limited to a couple dozen rounds at the range. My lack of confidence in myself was tempered, though, by my increased confidence in my new teammates. They were all so good that they'd help take care of us.

Then I met one of the other teams. They were dressed in the same sort of fancy outfits and goggles and had the same high-powered, expensive rifles.

I thought that everybody would be friendly, sort of like playing a game together. Really wrong about that too. There were people who had "history" and either ignored each other or gave glares or snarky comments. Some teams that had played against each other in competitions still had an edge, an attitude that bordered on hate.

One thing I wasn't surprised about was the male-to-female ratio. A few other women were there besides us, but basically it was 95 percent male and 5 percent female. We were more than a minority. We were a curiosity and the center of attention, getting looks and comments. Some of the comments were just strange, while others were rude, insulting and sexist.

One guy said there was "no room for women" in combat, and his buddies nodded, commenting that it was "a man's business." I pointed out that we were playing a game, and Ella added something like, If it was for men, then why was he there? That got his friends laughing at him, which got him angrier, which got him ranting even more about how we didn't "understand," how he didn't want to "kill women and children."

Ella said she'd have no problem hitting a "little boy" like him with a paintball and that she suspected his talking to her was the closest thing he'd ever had in the way of a relationship with a female who wasn't his sister or mother and that she assumed he still lived with his mother. Of course, that only escalated things further. Part of me wanted her to just shut up while the other part was cheering her on with "Go for it, Ella!"

That team and our team weren't supposed to be out at the same time. They either bribed or threatened another team and suddenly were scheduled to be our first opponents. That was just what I needed—psycho paintball killers who didn't like us. They started trash-talking to us and the rest of our team, going on about their "kills" and using all sorts of military language, and strutting around like they were actually going to war instead of playing paintball.

I asked one of the guys on our team—and they all seemed like genuinely nice guys—if any of those other guys had been in the military.

He laughed and said that people who had actually served in the military and been in combat hardly ever came to paintball places. He knew the guy Ella had accused of living with his mother, and it turned out he did live with her. Not only wasn't he ever in the military, but he worked in a shoe store—a women's shoe store. Maybe that explained his anger toward women.

Don't get me wrong. Most of the people we met were nice. Our team was made up of a chartered accountant, a couple of teachers, a firefighter and even a doctor—a pediatrician.

The final and biggest surprises weren't things I learned about other people, but things I learned about myself.

It all started building as we got ready to go out, as these guys, our "enemy," started turning up the comments. I knew it was just a game, just paintball. I knew nobody was really going to die. But that wasn't how it felt. Deep down in my monkey-brain cortex and in the pit of my gut I started to react. My stomach started gurgling, and I had to get to the toilet a couple of times before we got out there. My hands started sweating, and I felt hot. Then, as we got out there and the action started, it got much worse really fast.

I had a rush of adrenaline triggered by fear that caused my whole body to react. My hands began shaking, my body was sweating badly, and my heart was racing. It sparked a whole fight-or-flight response, and I wanted to run away screaming. I guess that was to be expected. What happened next wasn't.

Once it all started, there was no place to run. Flight was taken off the table, so fight took over. It started with that first "kill."

I was hiding behind a wall. Ella was just off to my side, also hiding. Neither of us had gotten off a shot because that would have meant sticking up our heads. Then this guy—the enemy—leaped over our wall, so close that he almost landed on top of me. I screamed, which startled him so much that he screamed too. He got off a round that splattered on the wall just over my left shoulder, and I reacted by falling away. But my finger was still on the trigger, and I hit him with six shots before he could react. That gave me a sense of relief, like I'd actually been saved from death, but there was something else—it produced a little rush of happiness.

I remember reading something in history class—a quote from Winston Churchill: Nothing in life is so exhilarating as to be shot at without result. *I'd been shot at without result. He'd missed. And then I hadn't missed. I'd splattered him with enough red paint that it looked like he'd really been shot. And it felt good. Better than good. It felt great. And I wanted to feel it again.*

In the end my final "kill" tally was eleven. Of course, I'd been killed three times myself, but that was a pretty good kill/death ratio—I didn't think I'd ever use that term in a sentence describing my activities.

After that first game, instead of hiding I went looking for targets. The rush of adrenaline seemed to make me think more clearly. I don't know how the same stuff that gave me sweats and shakes could lead to that, but it did.

My final kill in the last game was my favorite. We were playing a second game against our "friends." I was the one who gunned down Mr. Macho Bigmouth. I hit him with seven or eight rapid-fire bursts, including one shot that got him in the goggles, splattering red paint all over his face and hair. I guess that many shots was overkill, but it felt good.

His reaction was not quite as good. Despite being "dead," he decided to squeeze off a couple of rounds at me. Luckily, a judge saw it happen and gave him a one-month suspension from the facility. I was so proud that I didn't shoot him in the back of the head as he walked away. I was really, really tempted, but I didn't. I was better than that, better than him.

By the way, I'm not sure if that jerk is reading this, but if you are, you seriously need to get a life. A little less paintball, a trip to the barber and an occasional bath might change your life.

I stopped writing and thought about deleting the last bit. No, I was going to let it stand. I continued.

In the end we played five games against three different opponents. Our record was a perfect five for five. Afterward we sat around and talked. The guys gave us a formal invitation to become members of the Paintball Wizards! We were honored and thanked them, but we told them we were going away to college in a few weeks. Still, we talked about how we just might join them when we are home for the Christmas break.

Who would have thought it? Sophie Evans, Paintball Killer Queen!

DAY 68

Today I was a movie star. Okay, maybe that's pushing it a bit, but I was definitely in a movie. I won't be getting a credit and I didn't have a speaking part, but I did have a role. My role as written on the script was "girl in background walking through cafeteria."

Ella had arranged for us to be extras in a movie that was filming in town. It certainly wasn't a big movie—I'd never even heard of the stars, and it was being made for TV*—but still, it was a movie, and I was in it. It's supposed to be airing next spring, and it's called* Horror High School.

If you want to see us, you'll have to look carefully. You'll be able to see me and Ella in the background of the scene when the blood and guts happen in the cafeteria...well, the first time that happens. We're not in the second blood-and-guts scene in the cafeteria, which comes at the end of the movie. We were told that would be shot next week, but we'll be busy then—hopefully, doing another different.

I thought being an extra in a movie would be pretty exciting. It wasn't. It was boring. It was a whole lot of standing and sitting around and doing nothing except keeping quiet. And it looked like it was even worse for the stars. They did nothing in the scene, but they didn't get to go away. This one scene, which will probably be no longer than one minute long in the movie, took over six hours to do—and do again and again and again.

The best thing about being in a movie is the food. There is some sort of union rule about feeding actors, and they served us a big breakfast and a bigger lunch, and there were always snacks. I don't think it's going to be a really well-done movie, but nobody could argue about the quality of the food. It is a B movie at best, but A+ food for sure.

So now I've been in as many horror films as I've watched. I wish I'd been in this one before I'd seen the other one. Having watched how the whole thing is done made me realize there was nothing to worry about. Still, I'm never going to spend a night in a cabin in the woods. Or a school cafeteria.

DAY 69

Ella moved through the crowd, and I trailed behind her, pushing and shoving. She seemed to be able to pick her way through the packed audience better than I could. She didn't mind the pushing and shoving. It wasn't just that I was more polite but also that I didn't really want to make contact with the guys in the audience—and it was almost all guys here to hear this band. The place was packed, especially up by the stage, which Ella was moving toward.

I called to her to slow down, but there was no way she could hear me. I could hardly hear me. The music was pounding, the bass so overwhelming that I could feel it in my teeth. Could fillings be shaken loose? Suddenly I missed the sight and sound of the woman standing onstage, singing Adele badly to recorded music. Or the country-music crowd, which had seemed less threatening and much friendlier—and at least half of the country audience had been female. There were so few females in this audience, it felt like we were at paintball.

The song ended and the crowd erupted, jumping up and down, screaming, and waving and pumping their arms in the air. I used the little interlude between the cheering and the next song starting to try to get Ella's attention.

"Ella!" I screamed.

A couple of people right around me turned, but Ella didn't. She wasn't that far ahead, just a few rows. The music started again. There was only one way to catch her. I turned to the side, lowered a shoulder and shoved my way through. A couple of people gave me dirty looks, and one guy swore at me and then apologized when he realized I wasn't some dude. I was almost there...I reached out and grabbed Ella by the arm, spinning her around.

"Wait!" I screamed.

She nodded in agreement.

I yelled into her ear as the music pounded. "The crowd is too thick—we can't get any closer!" I wanted to ask, *Why would we want to get any closer?* because this music was a lot louder than it was good.

She nodded. Thank goodness. We were at a heavy metal concert. I'd have done my different whether we were in the third row or the thirtieth. We'd just stand here, bounce up and down and pretend to like the music until the concert was over and we could go home. Then I could see if I'd suffered any permanent hearing loss.

"There's only one way to get closer!" she yelled.

She tapped the shoulder of a gigantic guy standing directly in front of us. He leaned down and she said something to him. He broke into a laugh and nodded his head enthusiastically as she pointed at me. Why was she pointing at me, and why was he laughing? He turned and said something to his buddy—who was equally big. Then they picked up Ella, lifted her over their heads and passed her forward. She was body surfing over the crowd!

How would I ever catch her now that she was—the two guys grabbed me and lifted me off my feet. I screamed, but they couldn't hear me or didn't care. They spun me around, and now I was looking at the roof of the arena, lying on my back on top of the crowd with dozens of hands holding me aloft and passing me forward. I felt myself being jerked, flung forward, not so much surfing as breaking through the surf. I was helpless, out of control, unable to do anything. I stopped screaming and just bounced along, thinking that if going to a heavy metal concert was one different, crowd surfing should definitely count as a second.

DAY 70

I closed the door to my bedroom and joined Ella in front of my computer. In the quiet of the room the buzzing in my ears became louder. Remnants of the previous night's concert. My father had told me it would go away. Apparently, "back in the day" he'd gone to a few heavy metal concerts himself. He'd even taken my mother to a couple before she "tamed" him.

I was a little concerned that Ella had shooed me out of my room to begin with—she'd said something about loading a program onto my computer. That made me a little nervous, but then again, what didn't?

At Ella's feet was a large suitcase that she'd brought and forbidden me to look in. Now, dramatically, she undid the zipper.

I tried to reassure myself by thinking, How bad could this different be if it's in my room? Still, Ella seemed to have a way of making everything we'd done an adventure or an embarrassment or an embarrassing adventure.

"Your web camera does work, right?" Ella asked.

"Of course it works." An element of danger had been inserted into the equation.

"We can't follow our plan without a camera."

"So what exactly is the plan?" I asked. "And what does it have to do with that suitcase?"

"It has many things to do with it." She flipped open the top to reveal a bizarre combination of things.

"Is that a horse mask?" I asked.

"There are two horse masks." She reached down and grabbed them. "Here this one's for you." She handed it to me.

"Why would I want to wear a horse mask?"

"All I know is I'm going to wear mine. It's best that they don't just see two girls sitting in front of a computer."

"Who are *they*?"

"I have no idea whatsoever, which, of course, makes it so interesting."

Ella clicked a button, and the computer screen came to life.

"What is Chatroulette?" I asked.

"It's basically a way for us to have a conversation with people around the world."

"What people?"

"That's the roulette part of the equation. They could be any people, from anywhere," Ella said. "So here we—"

"Wait," I said, grabbing her hand as she was about to log in. "It says right there under the rules that we have to be eighteen to participate."

"You *are* eighteen, and I'm only two months away. It's not like they're going to check our birth certificates before we go online," Ella said. "Besides, *that* isn't the rule you should be worried about."

"What do you mean?"

"Read rule number three."

I scanned down and read *Broadcasting or offering nudity isn't allowed.*

"I don't think either of us is going to go breaking that rule," I said. Then I had a terrible thought. "Are we?"

"Of course not," she said. "The Internet is forever. Only an idiot does things like that."

I let out a sigh of relief.

"It isn't you or me that I'm worried about. Let's go."

"Wait, shouldn't we put on the horse—?"

Ella pushed the button, and the little screen in the corner of the computer went blank, then fuzzy and then came into focus. There were three guys not much older than us staring at the screen in what appeared to be a bedroom. It looked like they saw our image at the same time as we saw them, and they jumped up into the air yelling. They started talking, but it wasn't in English.

"What language are they speaking?" Ella asked.

"Spanish, Portuguese...I don't know."

They kept talking, louder, and waving their arms in the air.

"Stop!" Ella yelled. "Stop, right now!"

They muttered a little bit more but then shushed each other.

"Do any of you speak English?" she asked.

"Little, a little," one of them said.

"Good. What language do you speak?"

"Albanian."

"We are Albanian," a second added. "You?"

"American. We're American," I said.

They started hooting again and yelling out, "American! American!" until Ella shushed them again.

"You is very so beautiful!" one of them exclaimed.

"Mrs. America!" another yelled out.

"Yes," Ella said. "She is *Miss* America, and I am the first runner-up."

He yelled, "Beauty queens!" and then some words in his language, and they started cheering and talking among themselves.

"Actually," I said, "*she's* Miss America and I'm the first runner-up."

"It was a tie," Ella added.

"Do you...wish to be my betrothed?" he said.

"You want me to be your wife?" Ella asked.

"Yes, wife."

"Which one of us to which one of you?" Ella asked.

"Both of you to any," he said, and his friends nodded enthusiastically.

"That is certainly a wonderful offer," Ella said. "Don't you agree, Soph?"

"Yes, we're very, very honored."

"We're just going to have to think it over," Ella said. "We'll get back to you."

Ella hit the button, and they vanished.

"That was my first marriage proposal," I said.

"My third," Ella said. "Of course, the first was in kindergarten, and the second was from my crazy cousin Jimmy, but it's still nice to have options."

The screen came to life again. It was a girl, again about our age, and she was wearing a cat suit and had whiskers on her face. She looked Japanese.

"Hello, kitty," Ella said.

"Meow," she replied.

"Yes, and meow to you too," I offered.

She meowed again. And again and again.

"Yeah, we get it—you're a cat," Ella said.

She started hissing.

"An angry cat, apparently," I added.

"I got it covered." Ella bent down and rummaged in her suitcase. She pulled something out and slipped it over her head. It was a dog mask.

Ella started barking. The cat on the other end hissed even louder and started swatting at the screen. In response Ella growled, and the two of them went at it, fighting like cats and dogs—or, at least, a cat and a dog. I didn't want to be left out.

I pulled the horse mask on and started whinnying. Both the cat on the screen and the dog at my side stopped barking and growling and hissing and stared at me. Then at the same instant they both broke into laughter, and I started laughing as well.

"Goodbye, kitty," Ella said. Again she hit the Reset button, and the screen went blank.

"You have a dog mask *and* horse masks in your suitcase?"

"I try to never leave home without them. Those and lip gloss." Ella pulled off the dog mask and put on the second horse mask.

The screen came to life again. We saw a middle-aged man with a beard, holding a pad of paper.

"Hello, would you mind if I ask you two a few questions for a research paper I'm working on?" he asked.

Ella and I turned to each other. It was pretty hard to read her expression through the eyeholes of the mask, but I knew what I wanted to do. I turned back to the screen.

"Nay, nay," I said. This time I hit the button to change to another chat location.

"Well done," Ella said. "That horse mask suits you well."

Ella pulled off her mask, and I did the same.

The image on the screen started to materialize, but before we could see what was there some music came over the speakers. I recognized it instantly, even though I hated the song—"Wrecking Ball," by Miley Cyrus. Then there before our eyes was a guy swinging on what looked like a big blue exercise ball hanging by a big yellow rope from the ceiling of the room, and he was wearing only a diaper. Legs wrapped around the ball, he swung back and forth, singing along with the song. It was, well, mesmerizing, because it was so incredibly bizarre. There was only one thing to do. Ella and I starting singing along too.

That got the guy even more excited, and he started singing louder and swinging faster, and then the rope snapped and he plunged down and out of sight of the web camera! He bounced back to his feet almost instantly, still singing and, thank goodness, still wearing his diaper.

"Time to go," Ella said and exited us.

"I don't think I can ever hear that song again without thinking about that scene."

"That's better than having the regular video in your head," Ella said. She went back into the suitcase and pulled out a pair of tiaras. We slipped them on.

"Let's speak with English accents," I suggested.

"Certainly, duckie, we're members of the British royal family!"

"I guess we're both princesses this time."

She laughed, and I laughed with her.

A new screen emerged. Three girls wearing purple wigs and little bikinis were dancing and—wait. Those weren't girls. They were guys! They were bad dancers but incredibly enthusiastic. The only thing that would have made it better—or worse—was if they were riding on three swinging exercise balls.

❖ ❖ ❖

Ella and I had spent almost four hours traveling around the world. We'd gone from the bizarre to the ridiculous to the boring. We'd seen lots of different dances, music videos being reenacted, cardboard cut-outs of superheroes, and real cats sitting there staring at us. We'd had conversations with people in seven different countries. The final chat hadn't been much of a chat. It was simply some old creepy guy standing there naked. It had made me miss the diaper and wrecking ball.

It was late, and I was tired of being on the computer, but I had to post something. I felt like I owed it to the people who were following me. I logged onto Facebook as I started to hum "Wrecking Ball."

DAY 71

It had started with a conversation I had with an older woman the second time I worked at the food kitchen. It turned out she'd been volunteering there for almost fifteen years. Her name was Christena—she said to call her Chris. She was a retired teacher who was almost eighty-five years old. I couldn't believe she was that old. She moved quickly, told jokes, didn't need glasses to read things and seemed to have better hearing than I did. She treated everybody with such kindness and dignity—staff and volunteers and the people being served.

She'd talked to me about something she did once a month, and she'd invited me to go with her and the rest of the team. That's where I'd been tonight—and into the early, early morning. Part of me wanted to just go to sleep now, but I needed to put it up on my blog while it was still fresh.

We gathered just after 11:00 PM, meeting at the shelter and then going out in the van. It was me, my friend Chris, who is eighty-five years young, a driver named Brett and a fourth person, Julio. When I found out Julio was a police officer, I felt relieved. After all, when you're wandering through alleys in the middle of the night, a police officer is a good person to have along. Unless, of course, you're hanging out with a guy named Night Crawler and are doing street art. It would have been something to run into that guy again!

It turned out that Chris had been doing this for years. Julio had some experience as well, though going through the alleys usually meant arresting people, not giving out clothes and shoes and blankets. We were searching for homeless people who were so outside the system that they didn't go to shelters at night.

Brett would drop off the three of us at one end of an alley, then drive around and meet us at the other end. In the first few alleys all we saw were rats, cats and an extremely large raccoon that stared at us in a threatening way before it waddled away.

It wasn't until the fourth alley that we found some people. There were two of them. Julio saw them wedged in between a big dumpster and the wall of a building, lying on the pavement. At first I didn't realize that one of the two was a woman, because they were both in bulky clothing and woolen caps.

Chris offered them a place in the shelter—which they said they didn't want—and then we gave them some food, water and two blankets. They were grateful and shook our hands. That was the pattern I saw for the rest of the night. People were so grateful for the things we gave them—the most basic of things that humans need—food, water, warmth. It made me realize how much we all have in our lives and how so often we're not really grateful for it.

Going out in the middle of the night taught me that there are many people, unknown to me, invisible to almost everybody, who live their lives in the shadows. I also learned that there are wonderful people like Chris who want to help, who understand that street people are still people who need to be treated with dignity and respect.

DAY 73

"I'm home!" I yelled as I came into the house.

"Hey, honey!" my father yelled back. "We're in the kitchen."

It was suppertime, so I assumed he'd brought something home. Maybe it would be something good, but I wasn't counting on it.

Walking down the hall, I noticed that there weren't any dust bunnies in the corners and the floor wasn't dirty. There were no stains. In fact, it even *felt* clean under my feet. Had the dishwasher overflowed again?

Since I hadn't been allowed to clean anything all summer except my room, the whole place had slowly slid from clean to dirty to dirtier. I'd been afraid for what it would look like in six months. But not today—it was better. Had the two of them been cleaning?

Going toward the kitchen I smelled food—good food. I stopped in the kitchen doorway—stunned.

My father was at the stove, wearing a tall white chef's hat and a white apron that read *Kiss the Cook*. He was stirring the contents of a wok. I didn't realize he even knew we had one of those.

"I hope you're hungry."

"What are you doing?" I questioned.

"Isn't it a bit obvious?" Oliver said. He was wearing an apron too. His said *Be nice to me or I'll poison you*. Not quite as cute.

"We're making a chicken stir-fry," my father said.

"I see that. It smells tasty."

"It *is* tasty," Oliver said.

"And healthy, low-calorie and easy to make," my father added.

"But how do you know about stir-fries?"

"We got the recipe on the Internet," my father said. He held up his iPad. "Do you know there are recipes for everything on the Internet?"

"Yeah, this cooking thing is really easy," Oliver said. "You always made it sound like it was really hard."

"So now it's my fault nobody else cooked?"

"It's my fault," my father said. "But I'm trying. All we needed was the right attitude, the Internet and the right clothing. Just call me Chef."

"And I'm the sous chef," Oliver added.

"The what?"

"The sous chef. It's French, and it means the second in command after the head chef. I work under him, but mainly what it means is that I get to cut things up. Normally I'm not allowed to play with knives. Here I *have* to. I chopped up all the vegetables, and I even cut the chicken into strips."

“That’s impressive.”

“And do you know what’s even more impressive?” Oliver said. He held up his hands. “I still have the correct number of fingers.”

“You’re right, even more impressive.”

“Yeah, it probably would have taken away from the chicken part of the stir-fry if I’d sliced off a finger.”

“Not to mention the blood,” my father added. “We’re using a combination of soy and teriyaki sauces for the flavoring.”

“They were up in the cupboard,” Oliver added.

“I know. I bought them—back when I used to buy groceries.”

“We just ordered next week’s groceries,” Oliver added.

“We’re using an online delivery service,” my father explained.

“It’s really easy. Just ticking some boxes,” Oliver said. “I did most of it.”

“They even have prompts to help you plan meals and then reminders of things you should order to make those meals,” my father said.

“That’s amazing. I didn’t know about that.”

“So you are going to join us, aren’t you?”

“I’m looking forward to it. I have one more question. The house, well, it looks clean. When did you have time to do that as well as cook and order groceries?”

“I hired a cleaning person to come in once a week. Of course, we’ll still do the day-to-day things like dishes.”

“Believe me, I *know* how to use the dishwasher,” Oliver said.

I couldn’t help but laugh. He *had* figured that one out.

"I've also found a laundry service," my father said. "They charge by the pound."

"So you have somebody to clean the house, deliver groceries and do the laundry, and the two of you are cooking," I said.

"Yeah, that's right, you've been completely replaced," Oliver said.

"Nobody will ever replace our Sophie," my father said. "I just wish I'd known about these things years ago. That's my fault too."

"It's nobody's fault," I said. "I didn't know either."

"Now go wash up and join us for dinner."

I turned to leave before they could see the tears starting to come. I wasn't even sure why I felt like crying. Was it because they had replaced me? No, it was because my father had done what he'd said he was going to do. He'd done it for Oliver. And he'd done it for me.

DAY 75

We inched through the traffic. I looked out through the darkly tinted windows at the people crowding the street who peered in trying to see what celebrity was inside our stretch limousine. If they could have seen inside, they would have been disappointed. No Ryan Gosling. No co-stars or minor stars, or director or producer, or featured actor or even movie extra. Just Ella and me. It was my first time in a limo—which was a different all by itself—but certainly not *the* different for today.

We were both in elegant dresses, floor length and low cut, and mine was almost completely backless. We'd been loaned the dresses. To top them off, we'd also been loaned some genuine-looking costume jewelry, and our hair had been done professionally.

The gowns and shoes had come from the designer of the dress I'd modeled on the runway. The fake jewelry was from another one of my followers. The makeup artist who had made us zombies for the flash mob had done our makeup.

She was even better at that than she'd been with the zombie makeup. She actually hadn't used much less on us tonight than she had then. I almost hated to admit it, because it did sound rather vain, but we looked really good. I felt like I *was* a movie star. That was particularly important if any of this was going to work.

Technically we *were* actors, since we had been in a movie—*Horror High School*. I'd keep telling myself that, and if anybody asked, that's what I'd say. I wasn't a great liar, but I certainly could leave out parts that didn't fit.

Yes, Horror High School. *Well, yes, it's due for release this fall. I heard there was some Oscar buzz.*

Some part of me even thought it would be fun to try to bluff our way through with that line. That the idea of being discovered or confronted amused me more than it scared me was probably one of the biggest changes in me that all these differents had made.

"Are you nervous?" Ella asked.

"Not really. I'm thinking this is a combination of walking the runway and crashing the wedding."

Ella laughed. "That makes perfect sense, although try not to walk the red carpet the same way you did the runway, or they'll think you're insane."

"Being insane pretty well defines a lot of the things we've done this summer."

"Insanity might be useful, but we're going to rely on something else to help us get away with this," Ella said.

"Let me guess. We're going to act like we own the place."

"That goes without saying. We're also going to have something else."

Ella moved forward so she could lean over the partition separating us from the driver, Irene.

"Thanks so much for all of this," Ella said.

"It's my pleasure," Irene said. "I've been following your adventures on Twitter, and I wanted to help."

It no longer surprised me when somebody told me they were a follower or a friend, because I had so many of both, and so many of them were such nice people. I'd long ago capped out the five-thousand-friend limit on Facebook, and I had over eight thousand followers on Twitter and Instagram combined.

Ella had put out word that we needed a ride to the premiere, and the fancier, the better. You couldn't get any fancier than this car. It was a stretch Hummer that was probably worth as much as a small house. It wasn't just that I'd never ridden in anything like it, I didn't think I'd ever *seen* anything this fancy.

Irene turned and handed back some papers. "Here are your invitations."

Ella took them. "Thanks."

"You got us invitations!"

"They're not real," Irene said. "But they are authentically color-photocopied invitations."

"Where did you get the real one to copy in the first place?" Ella asked.

"Just about every limo and driver in the city has been hired for tonight's event, so I got a friend to borrow one and make copies."

"Again, thanks so much," I said.

"We're the next car in line," Irene said. "Can you two do something for me?"

"Anything!" I said.

"Just name it," Ella said.

"If you find yourself up close to that Ryan Gosling, could you give him a little kiss on the cheek from me? Tell him that Irene is ready to drive him anyplace he wants to go."

"I'll do that," Ella said. "And then I'll give him a bigger kiss from me."

"Hey, won't that make Shawn Mendes jealous?" I joked.

"All part of my long-term strategy. I think the best way to Shawn is through Ryan."

The car came to a stop, and the right-hand back door popped open. A tuxedoed gentleman as handsome as a movie star offered me a hand.

"Remember, smile and wave," Ella said. "Smile and wave."

A roar came from the crowd as I stepped out of the limo.

"Welcome to the red carpet," the tuxedoed man said as he released my hand.

"Good to be here, *again*," Ella said.

We started along the red carpet—it really *was* a red carpet. I felt a little wobbly on my high, high heels, and my dress was so tight that I could only take little steps. Ella and I linked arms, as neither of us felt very steady on our feet.

On both sides were waist-high metal fences, and behind those barriers stood a crush of people. They waved, screamed, took pictures and held out pens and pieces of paper, yelling for autographs.

"Obviously, they think we're somebody."

"We *are* somebody!" Ella exclaimed.

She reached over and grabbed one of the pieces of paper and a pen and signed it. People screamed, pushed forward against the fence to thrust out papers and autograph books and tried to take selfies of her and them. I grabbed one of the autograph books, signed my name and handed it back, then grabbed a second, and then a third. The more we signed, the more people pushed forward, trying to get our signatures. We took turns being in people's selfies or grabbed their phones, took pictures of each other and then handed the phones back to the owners. And the more we did it, the more people wanted us to do it. We'd created a little stampede of people on the other side of the barrier.

I decided it was best to start moving along before they figured out who we were—or who we *weren't*. I grabbed Ella by the arm and gave a little tug. She returned the autograph book she'd just signed, and the two of us continued along the walk.

Up ahead, just by the entrance, dozens of professional photographers were going crazy, flashes exploding as they took pictures of the people who had preceded us on the red carpet. Just in front of us was the co-star of the movie! We stopped to watch. She was being interviewed, four or five microphones thrust in her face and the throng of photographers surrounding her.

"Wouldn't it be amazing to be her?" Ella asked.

"I think it would be strange."

"As strange as ninety days of different?" Ella asked.

"Probably even stranger. Come on, we'll just slip around the side and—"

Another beautiful man in a tuxedo came up to us. "You're the next two up for interviews."

"Not us!" I protested. "We're just a couple of—"

"People who simply *live* to be interviewed!" Ella exclaimed. She grabbed me by the arm and started to drag me forward.

"Stop!" I yelled as I dug in my heels.

"Come on, Soph, this could be fun—and another different rolled into one!"

"It's not that I don't want to be interviewed. But I didn't dress like this to be dragged anywhere. We're going to strut over there like we really *do* own the place."

Arm in arm we strutted toward the interviewer, and the cameras started flashing, and the crowd cheered a little louder.

⁘ ⁘ ⁘

I pushed *Send* and the picture was posted to Twitter and Instagram. It was a lovely one of Ryan Gosling although he didn't even know I'd taken the picture. I'd taken it at the after party of the premiere. He was behind Ella, and I pretended to take a picture of her.

The picture made me smile. And judging from the likes and retweets and favors that instantly started to pile up, it was apparent that other people liked it a lot too.

DAY 77

"Are you all right?" he asked, his voice coming through the headset in my helmet.

"I'm...I'm good," I said into the little microphone. I was slouched down in the seat so that I couldn't see much of anything. I was trying hard to pretend I was sitting on the ground and not thousands of feet in the air. I had the GoPro strapped on, so I could see it all later even if I didn't see it now.

"You're doing well," the pilot offered reassuringly.

I didn't feel well. I didn't feel much—I was numb with fear.

"If you're feeling sick, remember you have the air-sickness bag right at your side."

I had one hand on it already. It wasn't like I had far to reach, or move, or stretch, wedged in the little cockpit of the glider. I was stuffed into the nose, and the pilot was behind me. Maybe that made it worse. He wasn't beside me or even in front of me, so I couldn't see him at all, and my seat was so tight that turning around was almost impossible.

All I could see was the Plexiglas canopy over my head, the little white nose extending in front of me and, beyond that, the thin metal cable that connected us to the plane—the plane that actually had an engine and was towing us into the sky. Above was a cluster of puffy white clouds. Around was mostly clear blue sky. Below us—well, I wasn't going to look there or even think there. I was just going to focus on the plane ahead of us. Originally my plan was to focus on nothing, to keep my eyes closed. I'd quickly found out that wouldn't work. The only way to keep my breakfast in my stomach was to keep my eyes open. Why had I eaten breakfast, and why hadn't it been dry cereal instead of bacon and eggs?

If I turned my head in either direction I could just catch a glimpse of the very tips of the wings. They were so long and thin and delicate, made of a fiberglass composite, and they were the only things keeping us in the air.

The pilot in the plane towing us and my pilot were chatting away. I understood some of the conversation, but they also used pilot terms I didn't understand—it was like a foreign language.

"What's our altitude?" my pilot asked.

"Seven thousand feet," said the other. "The winds are coming out of the north-northeast at fifteen knots."

"Do you have any reports of thermals on the horizon?" he asked.

Before we'd taken off, the pilot had explained that thermals were bands of hot, rising air that allowed the glider to float higher rather than simply gliding downward.

"I've had reports from other pilots that there are some significant thermals to the west."

"Roger that. We'll take a bearing in that direction. We're going to release in ten," my pilot said.

"Have a good flight."

"You ready for release?" my pilot asked.

I waited for the other pilot to answer.

"Sophie, are you ready for release?" my pilot asked again.

"Oh, sure, yeah, I guess."

"Be prepared for a sudden slowdown. You're going to feel it in your stomach."

"I'm ready." I wasn't, but what else could I say?

I heard a grinding sound, and then the line in front of us sailed away, trailing behind the other plane. At that same instant our glider slowed down, and I did feel it in my stomach. Being forewarned hadn't helped. Up ahead the other plane continued to pull away, and the roar of its engine faded to nothing. The only sound now was the whooshing of wind.

"I love this moment when I'm set free," my pilot said. "It's like letting a bird out of its cage, or I guess off its leash."

The glider banked to the side, and I screamed as I saw the ground beneath us on my left coming toward us!

"Sorry, I should have told you I was going to do that," my pilot said.

"I'm sorry for screaming."

"I'm trying to get us into a thermal," he said.

"I understand. I know."

"You know, one of the best things about a glider is you don't have to worry about engine failure. Regular planes need the thrust of the engine to overcome drag so they don't go down. With a glider we have much less drag, so the lift of the thermals keeps us aloft. If you think about it that way, you're much safer in a glider than you are in a plane with an engine."

"That's good to know," I said. I willed myself to believe it.

The glider continued to bank. I gathered enough courage to look over the edge of the cockpit to the ground below. There were large patches of green, crisscrossed by roads, and an occasional house or barn way down below. If I wasn't so scared I could have thought of it as beautiful.

"You're doing well," he said. "Much better than I did my first time."

"Really?"

"All I wanted to do was get back on the ground, safe and alive," he said.

"I was thinking the same thing. Maybe I'm not really doing any better than you did."

"I threw up," he said.

"I've been close," I said.

"I wasn't even close to the bag. It splattered all over my lap and then ran down my legs, all over my shoes and the floor. I don't think my pilot was very impressed."

"So far I've been able to hold it and—are we rising?"

"We caught a big thermal. I didn't think you'd notice," he said.

"It feels sort of like getting in an elevator."

"Thermals are like elevators for gliders, and today we're on an express to the penthouse! We could stay up here for hours."

"Hours?"

"Yeah, hours and hours, but if you want me to take you down right now, I will," he said.

I did want to get back down. I'd done my different, and it didn't matter if it was for ten minutes or ten hours. All I had to do was say, *Take me down*. I wasn't going to do that.

"I'm good for a while longer. Let's keep flying."

❖ ❖ ❖

I looked at the GoPro video I'd uploaded. It had already been viewed by a lot of people, and the comments were pretty positive. Funny, but the bumpy, bouncing footage of the ride seemed to be causing my stomach to flip more than the actual ride had. In the end, we'd been in the sky almost two hours. I couldn't really say I'd enjoyed it or would ever do it again, but I was glad I'd done it. One more different completed.

DAY 79

My father popped his head into my room. "So is there anything planned for today?"

I looked up from my books. "Not today. I have the day off."

"A day off would mean you weren't studying for courses you don't start for a couple more weeks."

"I meant the day off from differents. Ella's going with her father to a cousin's place out of town, so I'm free to study."

"Well, at least you'll have a quiet house for a few hours. Oliver's at a friend's place, and I'm heading out for a while."

"Where are you going?"

"Just out."

My father was so transparent, I could always tell when he was trying to hide something.

"Just out where?" I asked.

"I have a few places to go to."

"Where exactly are these few places you're going out to?"

"I'm going to go pick up some flowers."

There was only one reason he'd be getting flowers and only one place he'd be going with them. It was a place I hadn't been to for years and years.

"Do you want me to come with you?" I asked.

"To get flowers?"

"To take the flowers to Mom." The word *mom* caught in my throat and then sounded funny coming out. I never had any reason to say that word out loud anymore.

"But you don't ever go to..." He put a hand on my shoulder. "I really appreciate the offer, but you don't have to come with me. You really don't."

"I know I don't have to, but I want to. Maybe it's time."

❖ ❖ ❖

We drove in silence. The flowers for my mother were in the backseat. My father and I had exchanged polite, nothing-important kind of talk on the way to the greenhouse. It seemed buying the flowers had dried up our words even further, and now the silence was complete.

We had an unspoken rule in my house that we didn't talk much about my mother, and today we'd violated that rule by talking about her, buying her favorite flowers—daisies—and now driving to the cemetery.

My brother occasionally went with my father. I never had. In the beginning I'd always had an excuse, and finally my father stopped asking me.

The picture of my mother on my father's dresser in his bedroom was the only one that wasn't hidden away. Some were in albums in the buffet, and a lot were on an old computer that sat in my father's office, unused.

It took almost six months after her death for her clothing to get moved out of my father's bedroom—their bedroom. My father hadn't been able to do it. Finally my aunt Janice—Mom's sister—came over and did it. We left for the day, and when we came back the clothes were no longer in my father's room. They hadn't gone far though. They had been boxed and put down in the crawl space.

For years after that, when I'd go downstairs I could smell her. There were the remnants of her perfumes, which I still treasured, but there was something else, something that was the essence of who she was. The aroma stayed there for years and then slowly faded, and I could no longer smell it. But the clothes remained there.

"I'm still amazed that you went up in that glider," my father said, breaking the silence by talking about something safe.

"I'm still pretty amazed myself. It was really scary."

"It was very, very brave," he said. "It was almost as brave as coming to the cemetery today."

I was surprised. This wasn't just polite change-the-subject conversation.

"I don't feel so brave," I said as the cemetery appeared in the side window. My father slowed down and turned in through the gates.

"Do you remember being here the day of the funeral?" my father asked.

"I'll never forget." It had been seven years since that day—since I'd been here.

He pulled the car off to the side of the road and turned off the engine.

"We won't stay long," he said.

"We can stay as long as you want."

"I never stay long."

We got out of the car.

"Could I carry the flowers?" I asked.

"Of course."

I opened the door and pulled out the bouquet of flowers. They smelled good.

We walked among the headstones. I read little bits of information as we passed. Entire lives summed up in a few words.

"Here it is," he said as we stopped in front of her headstone. The largest carving was her name: Grace Elizabeth Evans. Hardly anybody had called her Grace. Her parents and my father had called her Gracie. Her sister had called her Spacie when she was too little to say *Gracie* and then kept on calling her that. Oliver had called her Mummy—he was only four when she passed—and I'd called her Mom. Elizabeth was her mother's name—my grandmother's.

Below the name were the dates marking the beginning and the end of her life. Thirty-eight years. So short. Just more than twice the length of my life. I'd never thought of it that way. I'd already lived almost half as many years as what my mother had lived in total. We'd passed headstones that showed people who had lived so much longer. How was any of this fair—to her, to my father, to my brother, to me?

Cheated of her in life, we were recorded in rock—*wife of Fred, mother of their beloved children Sophie and Oliver.* It felt strange to see my name etched into the stone, but I did feel beloved. She had made us all feel that way. Gently I leaned the flowers against the headstone.

"Could I ask you a question?" my father asked.

"Of course."

"Why did you never want to come here again to see your mother?"

"I *would* have come every day if I *could* have seen my mother," I snapped.

"It was insensitive of me to say it that way. I'm sorry."

"No, no, I'm the one who should be sorry. I shouldn't have been short with you."

My father wrapped an arm around my shoulders. It felt good.

"I know how much you miss her. How much we all miss her," he said.

There was so much I could have said, but the words in my throat were blocked, and I had tears in my eyes.

"She was so brave all the way through it," he said. "She was just concerned about us."

I nodded my head—that was all I could do. She had been brave. She hadn't complained, and I'd known she was worried about us.

"She would have been so proud of you, the way you've helped take care of your brother and me."

That was why I worked so hard, not to let her down.

"But she would have been even prouder of you these past few months," he said.

"She would have?"

"Definitely. Your mother had a real sense of adventure." He paused. "I'd like to think that she's up there looking down and smiling as she's watched you doing your differents."

It made me smile thinking about that.

"She would have been so happy to see you moving forward in your life," he said.

"When are you going to move forward?"

He looked as surprised by what I'd said as I was at saying it.

"You've never even been out on a date," I said.

"That would involve somebody wanting to date me," he said.

"Lots of people would date you."

"Yeah, I guess I am a real catch." He smiled.

"You are. So why haven't you?"

He shook his head. "You know your mother and I met in high school, right?"

"Eleventh grade, in the cafeteria."

He chuckled. "Me tripping over my big feet, falling flat on my face in front of everybody, showering my French fries onto her table."

"She told me."

"I'll tell you what she didn't know. I did it on purpose to meet her."

I knew something *he* didn't know. "Dad, she told me she *knew* you did it on purpose."

"She knew?"

I nodded. "She told me but asked me not to tell anybody. Especially not you."

My father chuckled again. "I should have known. She could always see right through me."

"That's not hard," I said. "You might be a great catch, but you're a terrible liar."

"Not enough practice. You know, from the first time I saw her I wanted to meet her. She was so beautiful and kind and fun. You know, you really remind me of her."

I'd been called kind and I'd been called beautiful. I'd also been called the opposite of fun.

"It's such a stereotype, you know, high-school sweethearts marrying," he said.

A stereotype I'd never know. I was through high school and through with my high-school boyfriend. I knew Luke wasn't the one. And looking back, I was lucky he'd realized it before I did.

"She always did seem to know what I was thinking better than I did." My father let out a big sigh. "I would have given my life for her."

"She knew that," I said in a whisper. "And she would have done the same for you."

"Or for either you or your brother. She loved you so much."

"I know that. But...don't you think she would have wanted you to move on?" I asked.

"I don't have to think because I know. Before she...well... she told me she wanted me to find somebody else and get married again and live happily ever after."

I knew that nobody lived happily ever after. "So why haven't you?"

"It's just that she was *it*. She was the one for me—the only one. I knew I'd never find another person to love the way I loved her—the way I *still* love her."

"I understand," I said. "But you still need to move forward."

He shook his head slowly. It looked like he wanted to say something, but now it was his words that didn't seem to be coming. I wrapped both of my arms around him, and he hugged me back, and we both started to sob.

❖ ❖ ❖

Today my different was maybe the hardest thing I've had to do. I went to the cemetery to put flowers on my mother's grave. The last time I was there was when she was buried seven years ago. The last time I gave her flowers was three days before she died. I'd picked them from our garden. I'm not sure of all the reasons why I haven't gone to the cemetery before today. I had the opportunity. My father still goes every couple of months. Maybe I was just too scared. Sometimes you can be so scared of dying that you become scared of living. I know I am not going to be scared anymore.

I put up one picture—of my mother's headstone—and added three words: **Loved and missed.**

DAY 80

In the beginning I found it strange and a little unsettling to go through my posts and read what "friends" who were really mainly strangers had to say. Almost all the comments were positive and supportive and often contained ideas for a new different. Ella mined those comments and connections continually to set up our adventures.

Of course, after that first negative comment I still felt a little apprehensive about what I might find. Somebody told me that the Internet was like giving everybody a stage and a megaphone and a belief that they had the right to say whatever they wanted to say and were so anonymous that they could say it freely. Things were said online that people would never say to someone's face. I hadn't had many negative comments, but they came occasionally, and I wondered when the next one would come and what it would be.

One of the things I'd learned through all this was how strongly I desired to please people, to be liked by them.

Even people I'd never met. Their opinions were more important than they should have been. I'd focus on the one person who didn't like me rather than the ninety-nine people who did. I just hoped everybody would be positive this time. Going to the cemetery had made me feel vulnerable and raw inside.

I started scrolling down. Lots of likes, thumbs up and positive posts were on my timeline. Nobody'd had anything negative to say. Thank goodness. I stopped at a long entry.

Hello, Sophie,

My name is Emily, and I'm thirteen years old and going into eighth grade in September. Although we're friends on Facebook, I know you don't know me. I know you because I've been following all the things you do. I've never written to you before, but I've retweeted and liked things. But today I wrote because of where you went yesterday and what you wrote.

What you don't know about me is that we have some things in common. My mother died too. It was three years ago. I was ten. I read about you going to the cemetery. I'd never been to my mother's grave since she died. I read what you did, and I asked my father to take me. We brought flowers just like you. It was so hard that I almost made my father stop before we got there. Then I thought about what you did and how brave you were, and I got braver. I'm glad I went. It was the right thing to do. I wouldn't have done it without you. Thank you for doing differents and helping me to do one myself.

Your friend,

Emily

I was stunned. I read the letter again. I had no idea of the impact I could have on a stranger. I thought back to all those years before and wished I'd had somebody to write to. Somebody who could write back. That's what I had to do. There was no choice. I had to write back, although I wasn't completely sure what I was going to say. It didn't matter—the words would come. I didn't need to think. I just had to write.

Thank you, Emily. I'm so sorry for your loss. I guess I know how it feels. Sometimes people will try to make you feel better by telling you they understand what you've gone through. They don't. Only people like us, who have lost a parent, can really know. I'm glad I helped you do what you did. I want you to know that your words make me feel braver too.

Your friend,

Sophie

DAY 81

I sat at the keyboard and tried to figure out what to write. It was a strange thing when a different had been embarrassing not only to do but even to write about. But the rules were the rules. It wasn't completely real until it had been acknowledged on social media. I'd never dreamed Ella would arrange this one and I had to give her full marks.

Okay, time to begin. I wondered what my father—or Luke—would think.

Today Ella and I went to the beach. The topless beach. As always I didn't know what was going to happen. I knew something was up when she told me we were going to the beach and was very, very specific that I had to wear a two-piece suit. Our day at the beach was far more than that. Thank goodness it wasn't actually a full day.

I knew something was bound to happen, but I wasn't prepared for this. We were just walking along and all of a sudden Ella removed her top! She turned around and said, "Your turn." I stammered and tried to answer, finally mumbling something about us getting arrested, and then she told me that we were on a designated topless beach. I looked around. There were hundreds of people. Some were lying on chairs, others on towels on the sand. Some were walking. Others were standing. Some were playing volleyball. All the women were topless.

It hadn't seemed like that good a day to go to the beach, because it was cloudy and threatening rain. Thank goodness for the clouds. Skin that has never seen the light of day would burn quickly. Slathering on suntan lotion didn't seem like nearly enough cover. I felt awkward and strange and like I stood out, like everybody would be staring at me. Nobody stared. Nobody cared. It was all just natural.

I guess we would have stayed longer if somebody hadn't noticed Ella pull out her phone to take some pictures. Instantly it was noticed and people got angry. Apparently it is both a topless and camera-less beach, and a couple of people yelled at her. That whole argument came to an end when there was a clap of thunder and a downpour of rain, and people grabbed their things and ran off the beach. I couldn't help but think I had a little help from above. Sorry there won't be any pictures posted from this one!

DAY 83

I saw the sign on the marquee—*The Amazing Alvin*—and looked over to Ella.

"A magician? We're going to see a magician?"

"Not *a* magician, an *amazing* magician, The Amazing Alvin."

I knew there'd be more to this than just seeing a magician. "Am I going to have to go up onstage as a volunteer?"

"Being a volunteer would be far, far too easy. Come."

She led me around the side of the building and through the door marked *Stage—Authorized Personnel Only*. We stepped inside and were met by a grim-faced security guard who questioned our admission. Why did every place like this have a slightly different version of the same guy? Did they all agree to look angry or constipated? Security guards and runway models.

Ella said a few words to him, and he broke into a friendly smile. He didn't look scary anymore. He offered a few kind words and then directed us to the right.

Okay, I wasn't going to be a volunteer, and I certainly wasn't the Amazing Alvin, so that left only one possible role.

Ella knocked on a dressing-room door.

"Come in," said a man's voice from the other side.

We entered. Sitting at a dressing table was a man wearing a tuxedo. Although he didn't look that amazing, I had to assume this was Alvin.

"The Amazing Alvin?" Ella asked.

"Depends if you're asking me or my agent or my three ex-wives," he said.

"There's nobody else in the room, so I guess you," Ella said.

He stood up—at least, as *up* as he had. He wasn't much taller than Ella and certainly not as tall as me.

"So are you going to be my extra assistant?" he asked Ella.

"Um, I have a feeling it's going to be me," I said.

"My goodness you're a long drink of water. Somebody as tall as you could make me look less amazing. When we're onstage, try to bend at the knees when you hand me things."

"I can do that."

"But there is a plus side to all of this. The costume features a rather short skirt, and with those legs it's going to look even shorter," he said.

"And how is that a plus?" I asked. He made me feel uncomfortable.

"Your job is to distract. If they're looking at you, they're less likely to see the trick." He looked me up and down. "You're going to be *quite* the distraction."

I didn't like the tone in his voice or the way he eyed me with what could only be described as a dirty-old-man leer.

Maybe I understood why there were numerous ex-Mrs. Amazing Alvins in the world.

"So how old are you?" he asked.

"I'll be seventeen on my next birthday," I lied.

"Oh...that's...unfortunate. I just assumed you were much older." He looked disappointed. I felt disgusted.

"Go next door and my regular assistant, Peggy, will help you with your costume."

❖ ❖ ❖

The place was pretty packed. There were more than four hundred people, but with the stage lights shining on us so brightly, I really couldn't see much of them. I knew they were there, though, because they oohed and aahed and cheered, and the one time I bent down too fast with my bottom toward the audience, it brought a whole different type of cheering. Thank goodness I only did that the one time. I learned to aim my bottom away from the audience.

Peggy had been The Amazing Alvin's assistant for almost ten years. She was younger than Alvin but certainly a lot older than me. Or the age my mother would have been. She said she didn't know how much longer she could continue to be his "lovely" assistant, but a combination of distance, heavy makeup, glittering costumes, Spanx and a push-up bra managed to keep the illusion alive. It somehow didn't seem fair that Alvin could be as old as dirt and still be a magician, but at some point she was going to be too old to be his assistant. But, as I'd found out over the years, fair didn't really mean that much sometimes. I also found out that Peggy was one of the former Mrs. Amazing Alvins. She explained that she was once young and stupid.

The Amazing Alvin was creepy, but a pretty good magician. He did all the classic tricks and even explained some of them to me. I was amazed at how simple some of them were. I'd share them in this blog, but I'm now bound by the magician's code of silence. To reveal any of the tricks could result in me being disappeared permanently.

Another different was done. And that was the real magic.

DAY 87

"I can't believe the summer is almost over," I said to Ella as we walked along.

"It's been pretty tremendous."

"Pretty amazing. I'm going to miss it."

"There's nothing to miss. Life is all about continuing to do new things. Just think—in five days you're going to move away from home and into residence. Are you excited or scared?"

"Both, I guess, but more excited than scared," I said.

"There's no part of you that should be scared," Ella said. "Think about everything you've done. Is going away to college anything compared to some of those things?"

"Aside from eating sherbet, I guess a lot of what I've done is a little more intense than frosh-week activities."

"You're going to be great. You *are* great," Ella said.

"So are you. When do you leave for school?"

"One day before you," Ella said. "I've got a long plane ride."

"I can't believe you're going to be that far away. I'm going to miss you so much."

"I'll miss you too, but there's Skype, Facebook, texts, tweets and phones, and we'll both be home for Thanksgiving. Okay, we're here," Ella said.

I looked at the sign over the store—*The Tat Cat*. What sort of place was—then my heart dropped. "Why are we in front of a tattoo parlor?"

"Raise your hand if you're getting a tattoo!" Ella grabbed me and raised my arm.

"I don't want a tattoo."

"You didn't want to do a lot of the stuff, but you did and were happy," she said.

I thought back to the glider, the runway, the karaoke, the snake, the roller coaster and all of the other things I'd done.

I nodded. "I'm glad I did all of them, but a tattoo? Isn't it permanent and painful?"

"I've heard it ranges from mildly uncomfortable to extremely painful, depending where on the body it's put. Face, neck, hands, feet, ankles and rib cage are the worst. Forearm, shoulder, calves and butt are the least painful."

"How do you know all of this?"

"Do you think I'd suggest you do something I didn't research thoroughly?"

"But what about things like hepatitis or—?"

"Got it covered." Ella pulled out a piece of paper. "This is the report from public health giving this tattoo parlor the highest scores on sanitation and practice in the city. I figured you'd like to see that before going inside."

"I guess it's good that this place won't give me a disease, but this is different than the other things I've done because it's forever."

"Soph, *everything* you've done is forever. Those experiences will always be part of you."

"But not visible for everybody to see."

"That's where you're wrong. Anybody who looks at you knows you're a different person than you were less than ninety days ago."

"Look, I don't even know what tattoo I'd get."

"It's already been selected, designed and arranged."

"It is?" I was almost too stunned to talk. "What am I getting?"

"That would spoil the surprise."

"You're not going to tell me?"

She shook her head. "You'll like it a lot. Have faith. In fact, you have to have so much faith that you don't even look at it while it's being done."

"You can't be serious."

"Completely, 100 percent serious. This is a total act of faith and a total loss of control. This is the ultimate test."

"Look, I just don't think this is such a great idea."

"You've come too far to back out now. Just sit back, relax and close your eyes. I've been told it's better not to look as they insert little needles into your arm thousands of times."

"You've found a way to make it even less attractive."

"I think it'll be more meaningful for you to see the design fully created rather than little by little as it emerges."

"So...just so I understand. You want me to get a tattoo, which I really don't want to get, and I don't get to choose what it is or even know what it is until it's already etched into me."

"Yes, that's what I'm asking you to do."

This couldn't be real.

"But I will tell you where it will be," Ella said. She took me by the hand again and turned my arm over. "Right here on your left forearm. It won't be big, but it will be where you'll be able to see it whenever you want."

I looked down at my arm—my un-inked arm—and thought about how much I didn't want to have anything there.

"Well?" Ella asked.

"I don't want to do it."

"But will you? You've trusted me for the whole summer. Will you trust me one last time?"

"I've already trusted you with my life. At least a few times."

"So?"

I hesitated before answering. "Let's go inside."

"That's my girl."

Ella opened the door, I stepped inside, and she closed the door behind me. The place looked deserted. It held some cabinets and six empty chairs, the sort that would be in a hair salon. In fact, it looked like a hair place.

"Hello!" Ella called out.

A curtain parted, and a woman covered with tattoos stepped out.

"Are you Elvira?" Ella asked.

"That's me. Are you Ella?"

"Yes, and this is your canvas for the day, the girl I told you about over the phone, my friend Sophie."

"She must be a very good friend to agree to do this without knowing what's being tattooed."

"Or a very trusting and stupid friend," I added.

"Or you could be all three of those at once. Have a seat," she said and gestured to one of the chairs.

Uneasily I settled into the big comfy seat. She pulled up a stool and sat down beside me.

"You are eighteen, right?" Elvira asked.

"Yes, just a few months ago."

"Excellent. If you were younger you'd either have to be accompanied by a parent or have a signed release."

I turned to Ella. "I hadn't even thought about it, but what's my father going to say about this?"

"I talked to him about it. He even knows the tattoo you're getting."

"He does?"

"Both he and your brother."

"Oliver knows and he didn't tell me?"

"He wanted to come along and get a tattoo as well. He wanted *This side up* to be tattooed upside down on his stomach."

"Idiot."

"He even did a rough version with a marker to show me and your dad. I'm shocked how well he can write on himself."

"Okay, this is all fascinating," Elvira said, although she didn't sound like she was finding it anything other than boring. "So left or right arm?"

"She's right-handed, so I think her left forearm would be better," Ella said.

Elvira pushed up the sleeve of my sweater to reveal the target of the ink.

"So, Sophie, just to confirm, you're agreeable to this happening, correct?" she asked.

I nodded. "Go ahead. Let's do it."

"I'm going to apply an antiseptic swab to sanitize it and then shave the site."

"You're going to shave my arm?"

"Just where the tat is going. Let's get started."

❖ ❖ ❖

Ella sat beside me, holding my hand, distracting me and keeping me looking away from where Elvira was working. I felt a series of painful punctures, followed by a soothing rub as she removed the excess ink. Part of me was tempted to peek at the design, but the biggest part just wanted to pretend it wasn't happening. Of course, the pain of the needles plunging into my skin and the whirring of the little machine made it impossible to ignore. What was it going to be?

"There, finished," Elvira said.

"Really?" I asked.

"I am unless you want me to do a second one."

"No! One is enough."

"Are you ready to see your tattoo?" Ella asked.

"Ready or not, I guess it's time."

I looked at my arm. There was one word. *Grace*. My mother's name. I burst into tears.

DAY 88

"How's your arm feeling?" Ella asked.

"It's sore." I pulled up the sleeve of my top to show her the spot on my arm protected by gauze, a bandage and elastic tape. Underneath was my tattoo—underneath was my mother. From now on, for the rest of my life, I would have Grace on my arm as well as in my heart.

"What did your father say when he saw it?"

"He didn't say much, but he did cry a lot. We both cried."

"I like that your father isn't afraid to show his emotions."

"He's always been that way." I thought a little bit. "What I didn't realize is how strong he is. He and my brother are going to do okay without me being here. I guess they don't need me as much as I thought."

"They need you. They just don't need you to be their mother. What they need is for you to do well at college. Speaking of which, I have a going-away present for you."

"You didn't have to do that! This whole summer has been one big present."

"I loved doing it, being part of it." She reached down, pulled a box out from under the chair and handed it to me.

"I feel bad that I didn't get anything for you," I said.

"Not necessary. This has been a present for me as much as it was for you."

I removed the lid. Inside was a book, and on the cover it read simply *Ninety Days of Different.*

"I've been working on it all summer. It's a book about your adventures."

"That's so amazing. I don't know what to say."

"Don't say, look."

I opened to the first page and there was a picture—taken by Ella with her phone—of me eating Wild 'n' Reckless sherbet. I laughed. "I had no idea that sherbet would predict the summer I was going to have."

I leafed through the book. Day by day, page by page, it showed pictures of my summer. It was like I was seeing things done by somebody else, or that I'd seen in a movie or TV show. But they were my adventures, I'd lived them, and there before my eyes was the photographic proof.

"You need to take this away with you to college," Ella said.

"Of course I will."

"I want you to look at it all the time so you can remember that you're not who you used to be, and that you're not yet the person you're going to become."

"I'm a work in progress. Like us all," I said.

"And that progress is made whenever we risk doing something different. You have to keep on doing different."

"Not every day, but I *will* keep doing different."

"Promise?"

"Promise."

I gave Ella a big hug. A thank-you hug. A sister hug. An almost-goodbye hug.

I couldn't promise every day, but I would keep trying new things—starting tomorrow.

DAY 90

I posted the picture on Instagram and Twitter. It wasn't fancy. It was a shot of my packed suitcases sitting beside the bed I'd slept in for almost all my life, the bed I was going to sleep in one more night before I left the next day for college. Of course, I'd be back at Thanksgiving and Christmas and the next summer, and who knew what would happen after college, but it was never going to be the same. This little room would always be my room. It would stay the same, but *I* was going to be different. There were lots and lots of differents ahead of me.

It was time for one final blog entry before I went to bed. I'd been thinking about it all the time I was packing. I'd written so many. I thought back to those first blogs, the first tweets, the first pictures, and how strange it had all felt. Was that even me? I hadn't just done the differents—I was different. I thought about how it all had gotten easier, becoming something I actually looked forward to.

This entry wasn't going to be so easy to write. Somehow I had to sum it all up, say something to all those people who had been following me along the way. Somehow I had to make sense of it all, and I wasn't sure I could. But I had to try.

Well, everybody, this is it. This is my last entry for the summer. Tomorrow, first thing in the morning, very early, I'm gone. My father is driving me to college. I'm a little bit nervous and a lot excited, and between the two I think I might not be able to sleep very well tonight. Please excuse me if this post is a little bit rambling, because that's how I'm feeling.

The last ninety days have been filled with so many adventures. They have been scary and unexpected and fun and amusing and improbable and seemingly impossible, but somehow they all happened.

I've learned to ride a mechanical bull, walk a runway, eat sushi, snack on sherbet, shoot a gun and dozens of other things. But it's not about the things I've learned to do but the things I've learned about me.

I've learned that I'm a paintball killer. I've learned what it's like to sit in the back of a police car in more ways than one. I've learned that I don't like heights but I can handle them. I've learned that snakes—even really big snakes—can be warm to the touch. I've learned that things that seem very scary aren't that scary once you're doing them and not scary at all once they're done. I've learned that there are things I never would have dreamed about doing that I'm definitely going to do again. I've learned that the impossible can become the possible to become the probable to become the inevitable to become the repeatable.

There was something else I'd learned. I let out a big sigh. It was something so important but also so personal that I didn't know if I could even write it down. It was hard enough to think some of these things to myself without having to share them with thousands and thousands of people. Wasn't it enough that I knew? I could always share what I thought with Ella and with my father. I didn't have to let "friends" who were strangers know, did I?

And then I thought of just one of those friends—Emily, that girl who had shared with me about the death of her mother. I could message her, but what about other people like Emily, whose circumstances I didn't know because I really didn't know them? What about all those people who'd gone out of their way to arrange things for me? All those people who'd written caring and supportive things to me? Didn't I owe them something more?

I'd answered every question simply by asking it. I had to let them all know. They deserved to know.

Eight years ago my mother got sick. I was ten years old, and I didn't understand anything about that. I just thought she couldn't be that sick and she'd just get better, because she was my mother. But she didn't. She got sicker and sicker until finally she died when I was eleven. My mother died and some part of me stopped living as well. I was too scared. I was forced to think about things I didn't have any answers for, to feel things I couldn't share with anybody, and there was nobody to talk to or ask. Nobody.

I thought about my father reading this entry. I didn't want to make him feel bad, like he'd let me down, because of course he'd never let me down. Just like my mother didn't let me down.

Of course there were people there for me—like my father and my aunt—but I couldn't talk to them, mainly because I didn't even know what to say or what I was feeling. It was all just so confusing and so frightening.

I remember standing there at the cemetery and being angry with my mother. How could she go away like that and leave me alone? She'd promised to get better and she hadn't. Aren't parents supposed to keep their word? Instead she just went and died. Thinking back to that day fills me with sadness. Not just because my mother died but because she didn't deserve my thinking like that. It wasn't her fault. Or my fault either.

On some strange level I had felt like her death was my fault. That somehow I should have been able to save her, or worse, that she left because I wasn't good enough. I must have been a bad kid, not good enough to deserve a mother. She didn't abandon me as much as she needed to get away from me.

Then I felt ashamed. Everybody else I knew had a mother and father. Not me. I wasn't good enough. I remember that first year after it happened, when the whole class made Mother's Day presents. It still hurts my heart. My teacher had to know my mother had died, but she didn't say anything. Maybe it was too hard for her. So along with the rest of the class I made a ceramic coffee mug that said World's Greatest Mother. *And I guess she was the world's greatest mother as far as I knew. I brought the mug home in my backpack and took it up to my room. I don't think my father ever knew. I guess —he will when he reads this. That mug still sits in the back of my closet in a box. Ungiven forever.*

I once read that when a parent dies, the child becomes afraid of dying. I wasn't afraid of dying. I was afraid of living. I lived in fear. Fear that something would happen to my father. Fear that somehow I wasn't good enough, that I had to try extra hard to be good. Fear that people would find out I wasn't good enough. Fear that I was going to fail.

This summer I've learned to conquer fear. Not fear of snakes or heights or speed or being embarrassed. I've learned not to be afraid of life, not to be afraid of trying, not to be afraid of failing and I guess, not to be afraid of living.

For this I owe all of you who followed and supported and arranged and accompanied me my greatest thanks. And to Ella...well, there are no words, but I know you know.

It's time to go to bed. Maybe to go to sleep. Tomorrow is a very important different.

DAY 91

"So everything is in your room," my father said. "Your roommate seems very nice."

"Very nice." I was sharing a dorm room with a girl named Becky, and she was friendly and nice. I would have loved for Ella to meet her—I would have loved for Ella to be my roommate instead of her. Poor Becky. It wasn't her fault, it was just that I was going to miss Ella so much—probably as much or even more than I was going to miss my father and brother.

Becky had just left to go to the bookstore to pick up some books, leaving my father and me alone. Of course, I'd already gotten my books back in June, planning to read them all before the school year started. I'd read some of them between the differents, and then my plans had gone in a whole new, unexpected direction. It wasn't so much that I didn't have the time as that I didn't have the same interest in doing it.

"Do you want me to take you out to lunch before I go?"

"Thanks, but there's a freshmen's meeting and meal in the residence at noon," I explained.

He looked at his watch. "That's less than an hour from now. That's not even enough time for a coffee."

"No, but don't you have to get back anyway? Doesn't Oliver have a soccer game at three?"

"I still have a bit of time."

Our dorm Resident Advisor had told us that the noon meal was partly for explaining the rules, partly to help us to start getting to know each other and mainly to get the "helicopter" parents to stop hovering and leave. I'd heard about helicopter parents, but I'd come to realize I'd been a helicopter daughter, partly because I hadn't known if my father was strong enough and partly because I'd been so afraid for myself and my brother if something were to happen to him. I'd protected him because I needed to be protected. He was sensitive and kind and nice, but he wasn't fragile.

My father had put together my new dresser and desk, helped put away my things, checked to make sure I had enough money and everything I needed. He didn't want to go, and I guess I didn't want him to leave either. I knew I could handle this different, but still, it was a *big* different. Away from home, at college, living in residence, away from everybody who had been my friends, away from my father and brother and Ella. Of course Ella and I had been trading texts all day. She was hilarious in texts.

On the top of my desk, right by my bed, was my precious memory book. I'd looked at it a dozen times over the past four days and been overwhelmed each time by the memories. The joys, the adventures, the seconds of pure terror and the lasting sense of satisfaction were all there in photographs as well as in my soul. Proof that I could do so much more than I'd ever thought I'd be capable of doing. Never again did I need to be afraid of different.

While I put away and arranged my clothes, my father leafed through the book. Of course, he'd been there for some of the adventures and knew about all of them, but he was still overwhelmed seeing the photos all together like that. What Ella had given me was the greatest present possible. Not the book, not even the differents, but what it all meant for me and my future. Did anyone ever have a friend as wonderful as her?

"You had a pretty amazing summer," my father said as he closed the book.

"The best summer of all time."

"And now it's over." He got to his feet. "I guess this is almost goodbye."

"Until Thanksgiving, and we're going to talk all the time with that phone plan you got me."

My father had surprised me with a new phone and an unlimited text, talk, long-distance and data plan so I could talk to anybody, anywhere, anytime. I could talk to Ella, far away across the country, and him and my brother, who were only a few hours away.

"Call if you need anything at all or if you just want to talk."

"And call me if you need anything."

He reached out and took my hand and looked directly into my eyes. "Sophie, we're going to miss you, but we're going to do fine without you. I've really started to like this whole cooking thing, and Oliver's been a great help. I have no problem turning on the stove."

"And no problem turning it off as well, right?"

"And turning it off. We'll do fine. You know that, right?"

I nodded. I knew he was right. There'd been bumps along the way, but in the end he'd proven that he *could* do it.

"I'm sorry for making you do more than you should have done at your age," he said.

"You didn't make me do anything."

"I made you feel like you had to take care of me instead of the other way around. I know I expected too much from you."

"No, you didn't do—"

He held up his hand to stop me. "Yes, I did. You've always been so strong, so capable." He turned my arm to expose the tattoo and placed one finger against it. "So much like your mother."

We were both very, very close to tears.

"Come on and walk me down to the car," he said.

He stepped out of my room and I followed, closing the door and checking to make sure it was locked. The hallway was alive with people, room doors open, people laughing and talking and getting to know other students, and saying goodbye to parents the way we were about to. Wordlessly my father and I went down the two flights of stairs.

Walking out the front door, we could see we weren't going to be alone in our goodbye here either. Parents and kids stood in little clumps. There were lots of tears being shed.

We stopped in front of our car.

"I was going to promise myself I wouldn't cry," my father said. "But I didn't want to make a promise I couldn't keep."

He wiped away the tears with the back of his hand.

"You know how much I love you, Sophie," he said as he wrapped his arms around me, and I hugged him back.

"And you know how much I love you."

He squeezed me a little tighter, and then we released each other. Simultaneously we each let out a big sigh and a shudder and then both giggled.

"You know I read your blog entry from last night," he said.

"I knew you would."

"That must have been hard to write."

"I've done lots of hard things."

"And I want to thank you for doing them."

"Thank me?"

"Yes. I'm going to try to listen to my very smart daughter. It's time for me to stop being afraid of living too." He paused. "Do you know how proud of you your mother would have been?"

I nodded my head ever so slightly. We hugged once again and then he climbed into the car, the window slid open, and he started the car.

"If there's anything you need, anything you want to talk about, you know I'm only a phone call and a drive away," he said. "I'd jump into the car at three in the morning, throw Oliver in the backseat, and be here if you needed me."

"I know that."

"Well, then, it's time. I'm not going to drive the route we came here by. I'm going to take another way home," he said. "It's time for a little different for me too."

He drove away, slowly at first, waving an arm out the window. I stood and watched until he rounded the corner and was gone. No, of course he wasn't gone—he was just heading home. I looked down at my arm, at my tattoo. He was still here with me the way my mother was still here. We'd all be okay. I just had to take the first steps toward okay.

I turned to head back to my residence, then stopped. I still had time before the meeting and meal. Despite my urge to retreat to my room, there really wasn't any need—it was all set up. Instead I'd take a walk around my new world—my different world. I knew there was nothing to worry about, nothing to fear, but still, here I was, alone. I took a deep breath and remembered all the things I needed to remember.

This was the start of an adventure, and I had to embrace that adventure. It was a beautiful day—my first day of college—and a little stroll around the quad seemed to be what was called for. The campus was gigantic. It was home to almost twenty-five thousand students, and it was time for me to get to know a little bit of it.

All around me was the bustling of the beginning. For some it was a rebeginning. They were coming back for a second or third or fourth year. But most who were here this early were just like me, beginning a new different. I could see that in their eyes and their expressions. Some looked confident. They'd already connected with friends or met new friends. Others looked lost—literally—studying campus maps with confused expressions. Others looked downright scared. I wanted to go up and reassure them that it was all going to be all right, maybe even wonderful, that they had nothing to fear, that different was to be embraced and not dreaded. Still, I wondered if I was wearing that same scared look.

"Sophie!"

I turned at the sound of my name. I didn't see anybody. The call might have been for somebody else named Sophie or—

"Sophie!"

I recognized the voice. It was Luke, waving his arm, running toward me, a big smile on his face. My old boyfriend, the one person on the whole campus that I knew and the one person I didn't want to run into—at least, not yet, not this soon, not today. I'd hoped it wouldn't happen for months. Really, on some level I'd hoped it would never happen.

"Soph, it's so great to see you!" he exclaimed, practically beaming as he stopped beside me. He was slightly out of breath, but his hair looked perfect.

"Yeah, good to see you too," I mumbled.

"It's pretty amazing here, isn't it?"

"Yeah, pretty amazing, at least the little I've seen of it."

"I've been here for a few days already. My parents dropped me off on Friday, and I've been here all weekend. I could show you around, if you like. I could even take you on a tour right now."

"Um, I have a freshmen's meeting in my residence in a few minutes. I better get going."

"Let me walk you back," he said.

I couldn't think of anything I wanted less, but what was I supposed to say? *Go away, drop dead, I'd hoped I'd never see you again?*

I turned toward my residence, and he fell into step beside me. It seemed so familiar, the way it used to be, except that we used to walk hand in hand. I drew my hand closer to myself, just in case they accidently brushed together or he tried to take it.

"I was hoping we'd run into each other," Luke said.

"It's such a huge place that I didn't think it would happen so quickly—or even at all."

"I have a confession to make," he said. "I wasn't leaving it to chance. I was heading to your residence right now to see if I could find you."

"How do you even know which residence is mine?"

"I looked it up in the campus directory. I hope you don't mind."

He looked slightly guilty but also pleased with himself. Did he think this was going to make me happy? Again, what was I supposed to say to that?

"I'd ask you how your summer was, but I already know," Luke said. "It was cool following you on Twitter and Instagram and reading your blog."

I wondered if he'd read my last post.

"I couldn't believe some of the stuff you did," he said.

"Well, I *did* those things, and sometimes I still have trouble believing it was me who did them."

"Rock climbing, gliding, being a runway model—you did some incredible things!"

"It was a pretty special summer."

"I'm not sure even *I* would have been brave enough to do all of them," he said.

I chuckled slightly. That sounded like Luke—a compliment to me hidden in one for himself.

"How did you even arrange some of those things?"

"I didn't. It's all Ella's doing. It was her and people we connected with on social."

"Ella never liked me very much, did she?"

"She didn't like you at *all*," I said. "But then again, she's always been a pretty good judge of people."

"I guess I deserve that," Luke said. "I said some things that weren't that nice."

"*That* nice?"

"Okay, maybe they were more than just not nice. But you have to remember that I also said you were smart and kind and beautiful...and you are all of those."

He flashed me a smile. That smile that had always worked so effectively in the past.

"Look, Soph, I know what I did was wrong and that the way I did it, the timing, well, it was even more wrong."

"I guess we can both agree on that."

"And I'd like to make it up to you. I'd like to change that." He paused and took a deep breath. "I was just thinking...this is hard to say. I've been so impressed, so amazed, by all the things you did this summer. Do you think...that maybe you and I could, well...?"

I was almost too stunned to complete his sentence. He couldn't really mean that, could he?

He shrugged his shoulders and turned the smile up another notch.

"You want us to get back together?" I asked.

He nodded. "Yeah. Sophie, do you think you could forgive me, that we could start over again, that we could be a couple again?"

In my head I ran through all the things I'd thought about saying to him over the past few months. I thought about the clever "ad-lib" lines I'd practiced. None of them fit, because I hadn't expected this.

"Well, Sophie, what do you think?" Luke asked.

And then I knew exactly what to say. "I've already done *this*," I said, gesturing toward him. "I'm going to do something *different*."

I turned and walked away to take the first step in my next different.

Recently named a member of the Order of Canada, ERIC WALTERS began writing in 1993 as a way to get his grade-five students interested in reading and writing. Eric has published almost a hundred novels and picture books. He is a tireless presenter, speaking to over 100,000 students per year in schools across the country. One of his most common themes involves the Canadian heroes featured in his novels and helping students to become aware of the greatness of their country. Eric is the co-founder of The Creation of Hope (www.creationofhope.com) an organization that provides for orphans and impoverished children in the Mbooni District of Kenya. He lives in Guelph, Ontario. For more information, visit www.ericwalters.net.

More BOLD YA from ORCA